THE ANDROIDS ARE COMING

Books by Robert Silverberg

The Masks of Time
The Time Hoppers
Hawksbill Station
To Live Again
Recalled to Life
Starman's Quest
Tower of Glass
Earthmen and Strangers *(editor)*
Voyagers in Time *(editor)*
Men and Machines *(editor)*
Tomorrow's Worlds *(editor)*
Revolt on Alpha C
Lost Race of Mars
Time of the Great Freeze
Conquerers from the Darkness
Planet of Death
The Gate of Worlds
The Calibrated Alligator
Needle in a Timestack
To Open the Sky
Thorns
Worlds of Maybe *(editor)*
Mind to Mind *(editor)*
The Science Fiction Bestiary *(editor)*
The Day the Sun Stood Still *(compiler)*
Beyond Control *(editor)*
Chains of the Sea *(compiler)*
Deep Space *(editor)*
Sundance and Other Science Fiction Stories
Mutants: Eleven Stories of Science Fiction (editor)
Threads of Time *(compiler)*
Sunrise on Mercury and Other Science Fiction Stories
Explorers of Space: Eight Stories of Science Fiction *(editor)*
Strange Gifts: Eight Stories of Science Fiction *(editor)*
The Aliens: Seven Stories of Science Fiction *(editor)*
The Crystal Ship: Three Original Novellas of Science Fiction *(editor)*
Earth Is the Strangest Planet: Ten Stories of Science Fiction *(editor)*
Trips in Time: Nine Stories of Science Fiction *(editor)*
The Edge of Space *(editor)*
Lost Worlds, Unknown Horizons: Nine Stories of Science Fiction *(editor)*

THE ANDROIDS ARE COMING

Seven Stories of Science Fiction
edited and with an introduction by
Robert Silverberg

ELSEVIER/NELSON BOOKS
New York

No character in this book is intended to represent any actual person; all the incidents of the story are entirely fictional in nature.

Library of Congress Cataloging in Publication Data

Main entry under title:

The Androids are coming.

   CONTENTS: Silverberg, R. Introduction.—Tubb, E. C.
The captain's dog.—Simak, C. D. Good night, Mr. James.—Asimov, I.
Evidence. [etc.]
   1. Science fiction, American.   I. Silverberg, Robert.
PZ1.A57265   [PS648.S3]   813'.0876   79-17457
ISBN 0-525-66672-9

Published in the United States by Elsevier/Nelson Books, a division of Elsevier-Dutton Publishing Company, Inc., New York. Published simultaneously in Don Mills, Ontario, by Thomas Nelson and Sons (Canada) Limited.

Printed in the U.S.A.   First edition
10   9   8   7   6   5   4   3   2   1

ACKNOWLEDGMENTS

"The Captain's Dog," by E. C. Tubb, copyright © 1958 by E. C. Tubb. Reprinted by permission of the E. J. Carnell Literary Agency.

"Good Night, Mr. James," by Clifford D. Simak, copyright 1951 by Galaxy Publishing Corporation. Reprinted by permission of the author's agent, Robert P. Mills, Ltd.

"Evidence," by Isaac Asimov, copyright 1946, © 1974, by Isaac Asimov. Reprinted by permission of the author.

"Made in U.S.A.," by J. T. McIntosh, copyright 1953 by J. T. McIntosh. Reprinted by permission of Blassingame, McCauley & Wood, agents for the author.

"The Electric Ant," by Philip K. Dick, copyright © 1969 by Mercury Press, Inc. Reprinted by permission of the author and his agents, Scott Meredith Literary Agency, Inc.

"The Golem," by Avram Davidson, copyright © 1955 by Fantasy House, Inc. Reprinted by permission of the author and his agent, Kirby McCauley, Ltd.

"Fondly Fahrenheit," by Alfred Bester, copyright 1954 by Mercury Press, Inc. and Alfred Bester. Reprinted by permission of the author.

CONTENTS

INTRODUCTION

The theme of the creation of synthetic humanlike life-forms is an old one in fiction. Greek myth tells us of the giant metal man Talos, built by the supreme craftsman Daedalus to guard the island of Crete. From the *Thousand and One Nights* comes the story of a beautiful—but deadly—mechanical dancer devised to amuse a foolish sultan. In medieval Prague was born the tale of the Golem, an artificial creature made of clay, brought to life by placing in its mouth a paper inscribed with the name of God. Mary Shelley, in the early nineteenth century, made use of a similar concept in her famous novel *Frankenstein*: a scientist assembles dead limbs and organs and, after two years of toil, succeeds in imparting the spark of life to his monstrous creature.

In modern science fiction, of course, there has been considerable exploration of the theme of artificial life, following two divergent paths. Strictly mechanical creatures, not necessarily human even in superficial appearance—automatons, thinking machines, organisms of metal—are known as *robots*. Those that more closely resemble humans, that are creatures of flesh and blood produced by chemical or biological means rather than merely assembled, are known as *androids*.

The derivations of these two basic terms are rather muddled, since the first robots of fiction were androids, and the first androids were robots. The term "robot" was coined by the Czech playwright Karel Capek in his *R.U.R.* of 1921, from the words *robota*, meaning "compulsory labor" and *robotnik*, "workman." But Capek's robots, although artificially constructed in a factory, were of human appearance. "Android" is an eighteenth-century word from the Greek, meaning "man-like," and in its first appearances in fiction was used to designate mechanical beings—as in Edward Page Mitchell's "The Tachypomp" (1874), where it was applied to a sort of intelligent calculating machine, or William Douglas O'Connor's "The Brazen Android" (1891), a story of a metal man in medieval England. But a clear distinction between the two terms has evolved today: robots are mechanical entities, androids are nearly or totally indistinguishable from human beings.

The distinction is an important one, because it has allowed for the examination of two distinct problems. Stories about robots permit an approach to the relationship between man and machine; the robot, which serves and sometimes dominates or even supplants humanity, becomes a metaphor for our entire roster of ingenious and perhaps dangerous labor-saving devices. But the android is something more intricate than an IBM typewriter on legs; it is *almost* human, human in all but birth, a second-class citizen summoned forth by scientific means to play some role appointed by its makers. The android story, therefore, can examine some of the most subtle and complex issues. The entire question of the moral standing of slavery can be looked at in a new light—for do we have the right to enslave creatures of flesh and blood, even though we have brought them into existence merely to serve us? We can look at the question of the relationship of humans and their gods, for surely we are like gods to those we have conjured into existence in our laboratories. And we can study the entire question of defining humanity, since androids *look* human, *act* human, *are* human in everything but the manner of their birth, and yet can legitimately be denied the status of true human beings.

The android concept is a fascinating one. It has long held my attention, and indeed I devoted an entire novel, *Tower of Glass* (1971) to an examination of some of the themes I have noted here. Unfortunately, there is no practical way to include even extracts from that book here; but an abundance of shorter works about androids exists, and I have selected seven of them, some playful, some very grim, to demonstrate some of the facets of the idea.

—ROBERT SILVERBERG

THE CAPTAIN'S DOG

E. C. Tubb

E. C. Tubb is a prolific and popular British science-fiction writer—his long list of published works stretches back to 1951, and he has been much honored in Europe for his storytelling accomplishments. In the United States he is best known, perhaps, for his "Dumarest" series of novels, a vast galaxy-spanning epic that must run to fifteen or sixteen volumes by now. His story here is one of his earlier works, one that shows the quiet and sensitive side of his writing—a gentle story of the interplay between human and android in a society of transitional attitudes.

We buried Andy beneath a tree which wept beside a river. It was a gentle place of flower-dotted sward rolling from the winding stream towards thick woods lowering on the horizon. The banks of the river were thick with fern and delicate moss, the green spears of water plants and the nodding solemnity of rushes. It was a peaceful place though not a silent one. The waters sang as they coursed over shining pebbles; their song merging with the sighing rustle of the branches of the weeping tree, the sibilant whisper of the nodding rushes. Insects added their sleepy drone to the natural symphony while butterflies, as brilliant as gems, danced in the scented air as they beat time to the music. It was a restful, tranquil, contented place, the whole basking in an eternal summer from the light of a swollen yellow sun.

It was not on Earth. There were no unspoiled places on Earth and on none of the parks would we have been permitted to desecrate the verdant turf. But it was not on Earth and here there were no property rights, no one to order us away, none to stop what we intended. So we ravaged the virgin soil and gouged out a hole six feet deep, six feet long and two feet wide. We spread the rich, black dirt around it and after we had placed our burden within, we filled it in again as best we might, patting it smooth and leaving a raw, ugly oblong sprawling its concave length beneath the branches of the tree. We filled it in and, awkwardly, waited for someone to say what we felt should be said.

"I—," said Hammond, and paused, sweat gleaming on his big face, the big, broad face with the deep-graven lines and the grim set of jaw, the face with the thin, tight mouth and the hard, uncompromising eyes. Hammond was a good captain as captains went. He could handle his crew and he could handle his ship and, according to his lights, was a fair and just man. Never before had I seen him at a disadvantage, but now he seemed to have trouble finding words.

"I," he said again, and this time managed to continue. "I guess that we all know what we owe to Andy, and I like to think that he knows how we feel." He dabbed at his forehead with a handkerchief, running it over his neck and behind his damp collar. "I like to think that he will be taken care of, wherever he may be at this moment. I hope so."

It was simple but it was sincere. Hammond didn't need words to say what he felt, his actions had already shown that. Starships do not usually stop off at virgin planets in order to bury their dead. Crewmen who die are usually dumped into space during transit; gone quick and forgotten quicker. It had taken much fuel and more time for Hammond to make this gesture and I respected him for it. So I said nothing, despite the irony, but instead looked at Clovis the engineer.

He was embarrassed, a man who did not know how to display emotion but who hid his feelings behind his gross bulk and a façade of coarse language. He shifted uncomfortably from one foot to another, glanced briefly to where the shuttle rocket waited to lift us back into space, then kicked absently at the mound around which we stood.

"He was a great guy," he said abruptly. And stared at Styman. "A damn good guy!"

Styman didn't argue. Styman never argued; Styman always stated facts and, if you disagreed with him, he would stare at you with a supercilious expression, as if you were too ignorant to waste time trying to convert. He was our navigator, a thin intellectual with an acid mouth and furtive eyes. His world was a world of facts and figures and, away from that world, he was out of his depth. He compensated for this by a sneering belittlement of the things which normal men hold in regard. But he did not sneer now, if he had I think I would have flung myself at his throat; instead he scowled and spoke the naked truth.

"We'll miss Andy," he said quickly. "We'll miss him a lot."

"You can say that again," I said thickly, and had to swallow before I could speak again. "I guess that he was the finest crewman I ever knew."

My eyes smarted, probably from the effects of the gum-scented air beneath the weeping tree, but I managed to stare at Bryant and, if the cynical, world-wise and world-weary doctor felt offended at a mere galley-captain giving him a silent order, he didn't show it. He didn't look at me, though. He just let his pouched eyes drift over the mound, the tree, the river and the flower-dotted sward. His veined nostrils dilated as he snuffed

the clean, sweet air of the place and, when he spoke, his voice
was surprisingly gentle.

"It's a nice place," he said. "A very nice place. Andy should
be happy here."

And that was the biggest irony of all.

I do not think that Andy ever knew what happiness was. If he
did, then he never experienced it. Once or twice, perhaps, he
may have snatched a brief contentment, but such interludes only
served to throw into greater contrast the grim misery of his daily
round. A man can be miserable and, in dreaming, find some
happiness, some anticipation, some hope for the future. Andy
had no anticipation, no hope and, if he could dream, then his
dreams were the worst kind of self-torment I know. A man,
incarcerated for life in a dank and isolated cell, can dream of
freedom and what he will do with it, but such dreams only serve
to increase his misery. Andy had no hope of freedom, ever, and
nothing he could do with it if he had it. Andy was not a man.
Andy was a male neuter manufactured in a laboratory. Andy
was an android.

You find them all over, the androids. They are of medium
height, hairless, slim-bodied and with dark, sad eyes. They
never smile and rarely speak and one looks so much like another
that they could be identical twins. They are, of course, all
springing from the same seed, all developed in the same environment, all built in the same way. When they emerge from their
plastic sacs they are as identical as peas in a pod. Later they gain
a slight individuality according to their treatment, but always
one will remind you of another.

They are the creatures who carry your baggage; who stand,
patiently waiting, for hours at a time while their mistress or
master goes shopping. They sweep the streets, clean the sewers,
polish your shoes and wait table. They do all the unpleasant

jobs, the ones no human wants to do, the ones which no human can economically perform. They have a number but no one remembers that. Some have fanciful names but most are known by the natural diminutive of their generic name. We had one aboard.

He came to us fresh from his sac and learned life in the prison of a starship. He never left the metal hull, not even when we touched down at a port of call, but remained on constant watch duty in the control room, releasing one of us for outside leave. He never felt the naked sun on his skin, smelled the sweet scent of growing things, watched a bird in flight or bathed in a stream. He never joined us in a tavern to drink and stare at women wriggling in seductive dances to the impassioned frenzy of drums. But once, returning unexpectedly, I found him reading a volume of verse I had in my galley.

"You're reading!" The discovery shook me so that I forgot my original impulse, which was to snatch the book from his hands and slap his face before kicking him from my sanctum as a punishment for interfering with my property.

"Yes, sir," he said. He called everyone "sir," from the captain down to the lowest stevedore. I noticed a thin film of sweat glistening on his face. "I'm sorry, sir."

He expected a beating, I knew that. He expected to be kicked and cursed like a dog which has messed on the mat or chewed the curtains. He had done wrong and he knew it and now he waited, dumbly, for whatever punishment I wished to give. Instead I took the book from his hands, glancing at what he had been reading.

"Do you like Oscar Wilde?" I commenced reading before he could answer.

> *We were as men who through a fen*
> *Of filthy darkness grope;*

We did not dare to breathe a prayer,
Or to give our anguish scope;
Something was dead in each of us,
And what was dead was Hope.

I looked up, feeling as strongly as before the impact of these grim lines. I looked up and stared directly in Andy's eyes. Sweat? Eyes do not sweat, not even the eyes of androids. But androids do not weep either; only humans do that.

"You shouldn't have come in here," I said. "You know that I don't allow anyone to mess about in my kitchen."

"I'm sorry, sir," he repeated. "But I was all alone and—" He paused, his eyes searching my face. "I didn't think that I was doing anything wrong, sir."

I remained silent, thinking, more shaken than I knew. It wasn't the fact that Andy could read which bothered me; he'd had his basic education before coming to us, it was what he had chosen to read which was important. It was as if a dog had suddenly commenced to talk. Its ability wouldn't make it human but, at the same time, it would no longer be wholly a dog.

"Make some coffee," I ordered sharply for the want of anything better to say. "Make it good and strong."

"Yes, sir." He leaped to obey and I sat down at the kitchen table, the book in my hands, the pages opening of their own accord to the *Ballad of Reading Goal*. Books only do that when they have frequently been opened at a special place and, much as I liked Oscar Wilde, I hadn't read that particular piece all that much. Andy? I glanced at him, busy at the stove, then dropped my eyes to the page and read the passage I had quoted. I read it again and then again and then once more and, each time I read it, the suspicion in my mind flickered to a brighter significance.

"Your coffee, sir." Andy was suddenly at my side, a steaming cup in his hand. He startled me; I had been far gone in thought and, at his words, I jumped, hitting the cup and sending the scalding coffee over my arm. Pain directed my instinctive response; I struck out, knocking the android to the floor, then pointed towards the door.

"Get out!" I snapped. "Clumsy fool! Get out and stay out!"

The blow was nothing new to him, the words even less, he had collected plenty of both in the past. He cringed and scuttled from the kitchen and, watching him go, I felt sick inside. No man should be so servile. No man should ever have allowed himself to be struck or spoken to like that without making an attempt to fight back.

But then, of course, Andy wasn't a man.

The burn wasn't painful, certainly not painful enough to merit medical treatment, and certainly not serious enough to seek it three days after the event had taken place. But the minor injury was an excuse. I wanted to talk about Andy and I wanted to do it with someone who should know all about androids and what made them what they were.

Bryant snorted as he examined the superficial injury. "What's the matter, Sam? Getting soft?" He leaned back in his chair, his pouched eyes sleepy looking. "The arm's all right and you know it."

"It hurts, Doctor." Of all the crew I was the only one who addressed Bryant by his correct title. To the others he was "Doc"; to Andy he was "Sir."

"Then slap some butter on it." The sleepy-looking eyes never left my face. "Are you going to talk about it now or leave it until later?"

"Talk about what, Doctor?"

"The real reason you came to see me." He gestured contemptuously towards my arm. "I'm not a fool, Sam. A man like you doesn't worry about a scald like that; not when he's col-

lected a dozen worse during the course of his trade." He tapped
my arm. "How and when?"

"Just before we took off. Andy tipped a cup of coffee over
me."

"I see." Bryant looked thoughtful. "So that's how he collected that swollen jaw. I'd begun to think Clovis was falling
into bad habits again." He didn't enlarge on what he'd just said
but I understood well enough. The engineer was a quick man
with his fists and tongue and the android had served as a
convenient whipping boy. Then, for no apparent reason, he'd
left Andy alone. It seemed that Bryant had been the reason.

"You like him, don't you, Doctor?" I blurted. "Andy, I
mean."

He shrugged, the pouched eyes cynical.

"I didn't mean to hit him like that." For some reason I felt
that it was important that Bryant should know the truth of the
matter. "It was just that the pain made me angry and I struck out
without thinking."

"That's the trouble with the human race," he said. "They
never stop to think." He sat, staring at something invisible on
the wall, or perhaps staring down the misty corridors of memory. He sat like that for a long time, almost as if he had forgotten
my presence, then he shuddered and pulled open a drawer in his
desk. "To hell with them!"

From the drawer he produced a bottle and a glass. He filled it,
drank, and then met my stare above the rim. For a moment he
hesitated, then produced a second glass and filled it to the brim.

"To the monkey men," he toasted, lifting his replenished
glass. "May they never stop to think for, if they do, then they
will find it impossible to live with their thoughts." He drank
and, though I did not wholly understand his meaning, I drank
with him. The liquor had forged a bond between us, a temporary
bond I had no doubt, but I took advantage of it while I could.

"I've been thinking," I said slowly. "About Andy and the rest of them."

"Don't think, Sam," said Bryant. "It can be dangerous."

"Perhaps." I stared into my empty glass, wondering just how to phrase what I wanted to say. Converse about androids to most people and they will regard you as soft or queer. "Just how different are they, Doctor? From us, I mean?"

"They have no souls," he said. "They are not born of women and so they have no soul."

"Is that all?" The answer didn't satisfy me. Bryant, I knew, was being cynical.

"What more do you want?" He reached for the bottle and helped himself, slopping a little of the spirit onto his desk. I suddenly realized that he was more than a little drunk. "Do you want an analogy? Take a normal baby, depilate him, castrate him, fix his navel with plastic surgery and, when he reaches maturity, you'll have an android. Does that satisfy you?"

"Is it true?"

"Medically speaking, yes." He wiped his mouth on the back of his hand. "Medically speaking there is no basic difference between an android and a human. I have already given you the spiritual difference."

"They have no souls." I shrugged; to me that was a small difference. Few of the men I have met could have laid claim to a soul and still fewer wanted to. But I did not argue the point. Bryant was not an authority on spiritual matters but he could answer something which had been troubling me. "Why are they gelded?"

"Gelded?" He frowned, then looked at me strangely. "That's an odd word for a cook to use. Where did you pick it up?"

"From books." I didn't want to go into the matter. Bryant didn't seem to want to leave it alone.

"Of course, I'd forgotten; you read a lot, don't you?"

"Why not? It helps to pass the time."

"So does card playing, conversation, the making of lace or the playing of chess." He glanced at me, an odd expression in his eyes. "But human company isn't good enough for you. You are lonely and so you read. You feel unwanted, insecure, and so you escape into the fantasy world of books." He shook his head at me. "Reading can be a dangerous pursuit, Sam. Men have ideas and they write them down so that other men can absorb them. Some men even act upon them. Revolutions have been caused that way."

"I'm no rebel," I said shortly.

"No?" Bryant raised his eyebrows a trifle. "Then why the interest in the android?"

"Just curiosity." I hesitated, knowing that my answer wasn't good enough, then decided to tell the truth. "I caught Andy reading one of my books. It—upset me a little."

"You see?" Bryant was more cynical than ever. "I told you reading was a dangerous pursuit." He shrugged. "If you weren't a bookworm then Andy couldn't have borrowed your property and you wouldn't have tried to break his jaw."

"I didn't hit him because of that. It was the pain from the spilled coffee."

Bryant didn't answer. He just sat at his desk, his pouched eyes staring at me as if I were a specimen beneath his microscope, his hand resting lightly on his bottle as if he were waiting for me to go so that he could help himself to another drink. But there was still something I wanted to know.

"Why are they gelded, the androids, I mean?"

"They aren't," he said promptly. "You've got hold of the wrong word. Gelding is what they do to horses. Castration is the medical term, or, no, that is what is done to men." He frowned as if considering the problem. "Neutering is what is done to androids. Neutering. But it means the same thing in the end.''

"But why? Why do they do it?''

And, then suddenly, I had the answer. I knew why all androids were neuter; they just had to be that way. Jealousy was part of it; the jealousy of old men for young, handsome androids, the jealousy of those without virility for those who are virile. But the main reason was superiority. A man, no matter how poverty-stricken or ugly, no matter how low his circumstances, could not help feeling superior to an android. It was the inbred superiority of a man towards a eunuch; a superiority which had all the tremendous force of race survival behind it. And the same reason also accounted for the fact that the androids were depilated; hair is also a masculine symbol.

But why we had androids at all was something I still had to learn.

It is an odd thing that it is possible to see something almost every day of your life and yet never really see it at all. Then, because of some accident, or because it is pointed out to you, your viewpoint changes just that little and you wonder how you could have been so blind for so long.

With me Andy was like that. I'd known him ever since he joined the ship and had used him more than most. A cook has a lot of work to do and he's usually working long after the others have finished. It was natural for me to pass a lot of that work on to the android; all the unpleasant work attendant upon the preparation and cleaning away of meals. And yet not once in all that time did I ever think of him as other than a machine.

The thought that he could ever get tired never occurred to me. I had ordered him to clean up and wash the kitchen, had left him plenty of work to do while I slept and then, when I had woken, kept him hard at it until some other member of the crew had demanded his services. And if he had ever faltered or had been slow I had cursed him, even struck him and never felt the slightest regret for having done so. Why should I? Can a machine feel fatigue or pain? But can a machine read poetry?

Andy had done that. But what really served to change my viewpoint wasn't so much the fact that he had been reading poetry but the nagging suspicion that he had not only read it but understood it. It could not have been accident that he had chosen that particular poem; the way the book had opened in my hands proved that he had read that verse often, how often I could only guess. But from that moment I ceased to regard him as a machine and began to think of him as an individual. And after I had spoken to Bryant I even began to think of him as a man.

Injustice does not normally trouble me; there is too much injustice in the universe, so much that it is accepted as a normal part of the scheme of things. Brutality has lost its power to tighten my stomach and send anger through my veins. I have seen much brutality and, by usage, have managed to isolate myself from it. The universe is as it is and the universe is too big a place for any one man to alter. And there are always books and books can be gentle things.

So, despite my changed viewpoint, I did not attempt to champion Andy or to protect him from his environment. True, I did ease off on his kitchen duties and forced myself to remember that perhaps he needed sleep as much as I, but aside from that I was content to study him as if he were a problem rather than a thing of hurtable flesh and blood. And, one shift, I discovered the reason why androids existed at all.

It was a little thing which did it, but how many discoveries have been caused through trifles? We had just eaten and Andy, as soft-footed as ever, had cleared the table so that we could sit in comfort, smoking and talking, relaxing as men must if they are to gain benefit from their food. Hammond wasn't with us, he always ate alone in the control room, but Clovis was there and

Styman and Bryant, each sitting at his own side of the table, with myself filling in the square.

The talk had drifted, I forgot about what, but suddenly something caught my attention.

"Captain's Dog?" I looked at Clovis. "Why did you call him that?"

"Freeman?" Clovis shrugged. "Well, that's what he was. A Captain's Dog." He chuckled. "Or he was until he jumped ship one touchdown and headed for the hills. I guess he figured that any sort of life was better than the one he had." He chuckled louder at my expression. "Don't you know what a Captain's Dog is?"

"No." I was curt, I had the feeling that Clovis was being funny at my expense. He laughed even louder as he read what I was thinking and jerked a thumb towards Styman.

"He'll tell you," he wheezed. "Tell him, Styman, about old Captain Delmayer and his dog."

Styman frowned, annoyed at being brought into the conversation, but he did as Clovis had asked.

"Captain Delmayer was one of the old-timers," he said. "I never met him myself, he was around long before my time, but he had a terrible temper, so bad that he'd had more than one incipient mutiny on his hands. You see, he used to flare up and when he did he'd hit out at the first man around."

"And he was a big man," chuckled Clovis, taking over. "His crew half-loved, half-hated his guts, but he could be generous and he was a fine captain in other ways, so they decided to do something about his temper. Anyway, to cut it short, they clubbed together and bought him a plastic dog. It was a big thing, so lifelike that you'd swear it was real, and they put it in the control room."

"Why?" I was interested.

"Some head doctor told them to do it, so they did. And it

worked fine! Whenever Delmayer blew his top he'd take a running kick at the dog and send it from one side of the room to the other. That eased his temper and kept the crew happy.'' Clovis chuckled again. ''It had to be a plastic dog, of course, old Delmayer was too fond of animals to hurt a real one—even if he could have found one able to stand more than one kick.'' He stared at my face. ''Something wrong?''

''No,'' I lied. ''Why did you call that man, Freeman I think you called him, a Captain's Dog?''

''Why?'' Clovis shrugged. ''The name just stuck, I guess. Anyone who didn't have the guts to stand up for himself used to be known as a Captain's Dog.'' He shrugged again. ''As far as I know they still are.''

He was wrong. Now they had a new name. And now I knew what the name was.

Once, while on a brief touchdown at one of the more civilized planets, an elderly woman stood at the exit of the landing field and passed out little slips of paper to all who passed. I don't suppose that more than one in a dozen even glanced at the slips and of that number only a tenth bothered to read what was written on them. In fact they were invitations to attend a meeting of the Purist League, a body of idealists who wanted to abolish the manufacture of androids. I had nothing better to do and so I went to the meeting.

The Purists claimed, and proved by graphs and figures, that there was no need for androids at all. Humans could breed as fast as desired and at a lower overall cost per unit than any android ever made. With mechanization the way it is, labor was no problem and so, demanded the Purists, why contaminate the human race with these artificial constructions of the scientists? Leaving aside that androids can't contaminate the human race any more than robots can, they had a good argument. It sounded logical and it even made sense. But they had forgotten the basic need of Mankind.

Bryant dropped into the galley one shift a little while after I had learned about the Captain's Dog. He sat down and toyed with the cup of coffee I gave him, staring about the kitchen and the row of books I keep above the stove. He nodded towards them.

"Still reading?"

"Of course." Here, in my own domain, I felt more at ease than I had when first I had questioned him about Andy.

"Andy? Is he reading too?"

"Yes." I felt myself becoming embarrassed and was angry at myself for it. "I let him borrow a book from time to time. Why not? Where's the harm?"

"In reading? No harm at all. It's in what he might read that the danger lies." Bryant, to my surprise, was very serious. "Such things as *The Declaration of Independence*. You know it? Or *Genesis*, or some of the philosophers. I warned you of the dangerous ideas men can obtain from books, remember?"

"Is Andy a man?" If I had hoped to shock him into a damaging admission I was to be disappointed.

"You know what Andy is," he said levelly. "I was watching your face when Clovis told you." He leaned forward, his veined nose and pouched eyes giving him a peculiar, almost inhuman expression. "Well?"

"I know," I admitted, and suddenly felt my stomach tightening as it had once before when I'd seen a wrongdoer being whipped to death for some minor crime. "But why? Why?"

"Androids are necessary," said Bryant heavily. "Androids, in one form or another, have always been necessary." He halted my protest with a gesture of his hand. "I know what you are going to say, that we've never had androids before, but stop and think about it for a moment. What makes an android a thing apart? Isn't it the fact that he isn't really human? And what would you call a man of another race? Another color? If you had clear ideas of what constituted a human, and you were human, than anything different from yourself couldn't be human, could it? And the same applies to beliefs, to religions and ideals. If others are different, then it doesn't really matter what you do to them. Because they aren't really human and the rules governing human conduct do not apply. And that isn't all.''

I didn't need him to tell me the rest. I didn't need him to point out that every civilization has its roots in a slave culture of one form or another and that so strong a heritage cannot be denied. And I knew that men were sadistic and that they couldn't help being that way even when paying lip service to an idea. Logic can prove that all men are created equal, but no logic in the universe can ever convince a man that every other man is as good as he is. And it is right that this should be so for men are not equal, no matter how they may have been born. Emotion and instinct can, quite often, be more correct than cold logic.

''We need a Captain's Dog.'' said Bryant. ''All of us. Something or someone to hit when we are hurt, to beat when we are beaten, to master when we have been mastered. We have to prove, to ourselves at least, that we are better than someone else, or something else.''

''In this day and age?'' I didn't elaborate the point but my eyes drifted over the metal of the ship in which we sat.

''In any day and age,'' said Bryant. ''Men haven't progressed, Sam, not as we sometimes like to think we have. We have technological toys and we have managed to develop a conscience, but that's about all. Deep down inside we are still the primitive and, if we can still the pangs of conscience, we can be as hard and as cruel as any insane animal.''

He was right of course. I knew—who better?—that civilization had progressed beneath a system which has accustomed people to being kicked by those above. Civilization has been a ladder which could only be climbed by a ruthless disregard for anything and anyone but self and, again, it was right that this should be so for, without such competition, Man could never have progressed beyond the cave. And Man is what he is; alter his way of life, his mental, instinctive outlook on life and he will no longer be Man.

So we have our system and our system works and, if such a system makes life a living hell for those on the bottom rung of the ladder, than that is the price we must pay. But we have a conscience too, and a growing awareness of the humanity of Man, and slavery is no longer to be tolerated. So we compromised. Add another rung to the ladder and so lift all humans to a point where any and everyone has something to kick.

Give all humanity an artificial Captain's Dog.

Things were not the same after my talk with Bryant. Not the same, that is, for me, though the others continued just as before, using Andy as a convenient mechanism, using him to vent their spite and their frustration at each other. A starship is a boring place with little to do for long periods and tiny feuds boiled between the crew. Styman had his knuckles rapped by Hammond, he was a hundredth of a degree off course, and kicked Andy viciously on his way to the dining room, kicking Hammond in proxy and so easing his soul. He looked startled as I grabbed his arm.

"Did you have to do that?"

"Do what?" he was genuinely baffled. "What the hell are you talking about?"

"Did you have to kick Andy like that?"

"That's my business." He looked down at my hand where it gripped his arm. "Get your hand off my arm, Sam. I don't like to be handled."

I hesitated, trying to control the anger which had tightened my stomach, knowing that I had no real justification for such anger. How I felt towards Andy was my business. It was something personal and I could not expect others to feel the same way. I released Styman's arm and stepped towards the kitchen.

"Just learn to control yourself a little," I warned. I could not help but make the warning. "Andy's no dog to be kicked around." I entered the kitchen and had crossed to the stove when I became aware that Styman had followed me.

"Just what did you mean by that, Sam?" His thin mouth was pinched together, a slit in the weak contours of his face.

"What I said." His eyes warned me, I had seen such eyes before, and I knew Styman was boiling with rage. He had been in a temper when he'd left Hammond; he had tried to vent it by kicking Andy and I had interfered. Now his rage had transferred itself to me.

"Andy's a thing," he said deliberately. "A collection of chemicals brewed together in a vat. He isn't human and you know it. Why the sudden interest?"

"That's my business." I took a deep breath. "Just leave him alone."

"Why?"

"Never mind why. You just do as I say."

My control was slipping and I knew it. Championing the weak is, I know, a waste of time. The strong despise you for it and the weak are rarely grateful but, waste of time or not, this was something which I had to do. It had become a personal issue between me and Styman and, deep inside me, I knew the reason why. For a long time now I had thought of Andy as a man, not as a thing, and inevitably, I had ceased to ill-treat him. I liked Andy; I did not like Styman, and the android had become merely an excuse to vent my own dislike.

And Styman did not like me.

"You should see Bryant," he said coldly. "I believe that there is a word for those afflicted in a certain, peculiar way."

"I don't want any broken-down calculator to tell me what to do," I said, and from the way his thin mouth tightened I knew that I was scratching at his vulnerable point. "Go back to your books, little man, and leave real things to those who can understand them."

"I can understand one thing well enough," he said coldly. He glanced around the kitchen, his nostrils flaring as if he smelt a bad odor. "I can understand dirt. This place stinks of androids."

We all have our weaknesses and it was his turn to score. We were being childish, of course, in what we were saying to each other, but since when have men in anger been anything else?

"If you have any complaints," I said, "take them to Hammond. In the meantime get out of my kitchen and stay out."

"I'll go in my own good time." Styman glanced around again, wanting to hurt me but not knowing quite how to do it. He sneered as he saw my books. "You and that thing make quite a cozy pair, don't you? Locked up in here at all hours reading that trash and staring into each other's eyes." He sneered again. "No wonder you don't want to see your darling get hurt."

I am fat and bald and not so young as I was, and violence is something I do not like. But there are some things I will not stand, not even from the Captain himself, and Styman had gone too far. He knew it. I saw his eyes dilate and his face go slack with fear as I stepped towards him and he cringed, his hands thrusting at me, palms flat like the hands of a woman.

"No!" he whispered. "Please God, no!"

"Are you crazy?" It was Bryant, thrusting himself between us like a wall of flesh, his hand gripping my right wrist. "Drop it, you fool! Drop it!"

I halted, staring down, my breath sobbing in my throat and, for the first time, realized that I had snatched up the big knife I use for kitchen work. Had Bryant not interfered I would have plunged it into Styman's stomach and not even been aware of what I was doing.

"He would have killed me," whimpered the navigator. "I could see it in his eyes. He would have killed me."

And then something happened which made all that had gone before of no importance whatsoever.

Starships are big things; they have to be in order that their pay-load capacity can justify the expense of operation but, big as they are, they have their Achilles heel. Every part of a starship can be maintained and repaired by its crew except one and that one part depends on remote control and automatic manipulation. An atomic pile is something no one has yet learned to live with; not unless there is thick shielding between it and its operator, and rarely, fortunately rarely, does something go wrong. But when it does, then death is immediate.

The sound of the alarm siren killed our futile quarrel as though it had never been. Clovis, his face white and taut, came running towards us, Hammond close behind. They didn't need to say anything; the siren was plain enough, but Clovis explained anyway.

"The automatics have gone out of kilter," he wheezed. "The dampening rods are out and the Röntgen count is rising."

"How fast?" Bryant was concerned about the medical aspects.

"Too fast. We've maybe ten minutes, maybe less." Clovis wiped sweat from his forehead, forgetting even to curse in the emergency.

"What went wrong?" Styman was more practical. Hammond answered him as he joined us.

"From what I can discover one of the brace-rods has snapped, probably because of metal fatigue. In falling it threw out the dampers and jammed them open against the remote controls." He passed a hand over his face, closing his eyes for a moment as if the light hurt them. "A broken rod," he said. "A simple thing like that."

"We can fix it," said Clovis. "But someone will have to go in there to do it." And then he fell silent while we each watched the others.

I do not know how many books I have read, thousands probably, and I am fully aware of the way men are supposed to act when faced with a situation such as ours. In books the hero always volunteers to save the lives of the rest. In books—but not in real life.

In real life, existence is too sweet, the mere act of breathing too important for heroics. Old as I am, useless though I may be, yet life is still sweet. There are books still to read, poetry still to relish, a thousand light-years still to traverse, and if life is important to me it is no less important to the others. And so we stood there, watching each other, while time seemed to have slowed so that each heartbeat became a separate, discernible function of our bodies.

"We could draw straws," suggested Clovis. "Short man goes in."

"No," said Hammond. "We can't do that." He passed his hand over his face again, and again closed his eyes and this time I knew why he made the gesture. For there could be no argument as to who had to venture close to the pile and die so that others might live. Failing a volunteer, the safety of the ship was the Captain's responsibility. Hammond was going to die, and soon, and he knew it. And his gesture was his way of saying good-bye to the present. And though we grieved for him, none of us was willing to take his place. None of us, that is, with one exception.

"I will go," said Andy, and it showed his state of mind that not only did he volunteer to speak unbidden, but omitted any form of title. "Tell me what to do and I will do it."

He stood beside me and a little behind; until he spoke none of us had suspected his presence. He had joined us as soft-footed as ever and now he stood, not smiling, not frowning, as emotionless as usual, waiting for our reply to his amazing offer. I do not know what he expected our reaction to be, I could not even guess, but one thing is certain, he did not expect no reaction at all.

"I won't wear a suit," said Hammond, ignoring the android. "The protection isn't enough and it will slow me down. I'll dive in, shift the broken rod and get out again as fast as I can. Bryant, you'll stand by to do what you can. Styman, you'll be in command until a new Captain can be appointed." He hesitated. "We have a little time before the danger peak is reached. There are one or two matters I wish to attend to before—" He took a deep breath, not finishing the sentence. "I will be back in good time." He turned and walked back towards the control room, walking proudly as became a man.

"I don't understand, sir." Andy plucked at my arm. "I said that I would go; why doesn't he let me?"

I stared at him as he stood beside me, so insignificant that, in a moment of crisis, no one had even been aware of his presence, and I knew that I could never make him understand. How can you tell a dog a dog's duties? How can you explain to something which has always been on the bottom rung that those on the top have more than just the best things in the universe? They have authority and they have responsibility, but they also have pride. And when it comes to the point a man does not expect a dog to volunteer to do his master's duty.

"He will die in there, won't he, sir?" Andy nodded towards the engine room.

"Yes."

"He will cease to be," he murmured. "All this," and his eyes took in the entire vessel and his existence aboard it, "all this will cease to be. It will be ended, over, finished forever. Does he want that?''

"No,'' I said. ''But unless he does it we will all die.'' I forestalled his next question. ''And he will never permit you to take his place. Never.''

"To die,'' he murmered. ''To sleep, no more—'' And then he was gone, running away from me down the corridor towards the sealed door of the engine room, racing past Clovis and Bryant and the startled face of Styman, running with a patter of feet while the words of the unhappy Dane echoed in my ears.

I tried to catch him; would have done so had not Bryant caught my arm and dragged me back. Even then I think I would have reached him in time had not the doctor slapped my face and called to the others to restrain me. They held me tight between them so that I could do nothing but watch and curse helplessly while Andy undogged the external door and ran inside to his death.

"The fool!'' I fought to free my arms so that they had trouble in keeping on their feet. ''He'll die in there! Die!''

"Is that bad?'' Bryant rested his fingers on my throat. ''Relax now, Sam or I'll squeeze your carotids and black you out.''

"But—''

"But nothing.'' He nodded to the others and they eased their grasp on my arms. ''You and your books! I warned you about letting Andy read but you wouldn't listen. Did you think that you were being kind? Did you think that by showing him all the things that he missed, that he could never enjoy, that you were doing him a favor?'' The disgust in his voice startled me so that I forgot to struggle and stood limp, shocked by the sudden realization of the truth that was being shown to me.

"Dying is the kindest thing that could happen to him,'' said Bryant heavily. ''Why else do you think I held you back?'' And he stepped away from me as the others released my arms.

And so we stood, waiting, Hammond too, when he finally joined us ready for death and finding instead a hope of life. We waited while a man-made thing passed through the shielding into the invisible flame of atomic pile. Waited while our nerves crawled and our hearts slowed and time hung in an eternity of emptiness. Waited until Andy finally emerged into sight again, falling into the corridor with the last of his strength, his eyes fixed on mine until the last. And then we had to wait some more while the radiation counters eased from the red, waiting until his body cooled so that we could enclose him in a plastic bag without fear of the invisible death he carried.

And, while we waited, who knew what thoughts passed through the others' minds? Regret at unkindness done and now irredeemable? Guilt at unthinking brutality? Sorrow at treatment, undeserved and yet received in full measure from the hands of those who boast that they are made in the image of their Creator?

Whatever we thought, we tried to make up for all that had been done in the end. And so, we halted at a virgin planet and buried Andy beneath a tree which wept beside a river in a gentle place of flower-dotted sward and drifting butterflies. More than that we could not do, for the highest honor men can pay is to bury a stranger as one of their own. And it is a comfort to know that, at the last, we regarded Andy as a man.

Even though it was far too late by then to do him any good.

GOOD NIGHT, MR. JAMES

Clifford D. Simak

That mild-mannered Minnesotan, Cliff Simak, speaks softly and employs a quiet, low-key style of writing. But in his case style is not necessarily a clue to content, for in his quiet way he often tells complex and tricky stories that zig and zag into areas altogether unexpected. As, for example, the present item, which starts as one sort of story, shortly becomes something else entirely, and by easy stages leads the astonished reader toward a terrifying climax.

I

He came alive from nothing. He became aware from un-awareness.

He smelled the air of the night and heard the trees whispering on the embankment above him and the breeze that had set the trees to whispering came down to him and felt him over with soft and tender fingers, for all the world as if it were examining him for broken bones or contusions and abrasions.

He sat up and put both his palms down upon the ground beside him to help him sit erect and stared into the darkness. Memory came slowly and when it came it was incomplete and answered nothing.

His name was Henderson James and he was a human being and he was sitting somewhere on a planet that was called the Earth. He was thirty-six years old and he was, in his own way, famous, and comfortably well off. He lived in an old ancestral home on Summit Avenue, which was a respectable address even if it had lost some of its smartness in the last twenty years or so.

On the road above the slope of the embankment a car went past with its tires whining on the pavement, and for a moment its headlights made the treetops glow. Far away, muted by the distance, a whistle cried out. And somewhere else a dog was barking with a flat viciousness.

His name was Henderson James, and if that was true, why was he here? Why should Henderson James be sitting on the slope of an embankment, listening to the wind in the trees and to a wailing whistle and a barking dog? Something had gone wrong, some incident that, if he could but remember it, might answer all his questions.

There was a job to do.

He sat and stared into the night and found that he was shivering, although there was no reason why he should, for the night was not that cold. Beyond the embankment he heard the sounds of a city late at night, the distant whine of the speeding car and the far-off wind-broken screaming of a siren. Once a man walked along a street close by and James sat listening to his footsteps until they had faded out of hearing.

Something had happened and there was a job to do, a job that he had been doing, a job that somehow had been strangely interrupted by the inexplicable incident which had left him lying here on this embankment.

He checked himself. Clothing . . . shorts and shirt, strong shoes, his wristwatch and the gun in the holster at his side.

A gun?

The job involved a gun.

He had been hunting in the city, hunting something that required a gun. Something that was prowling in the night and a thing that must be killed.

Then he knew the answer, but even as he knew it he sat for a moment wondering at the strange, methodical, step-by-step progression of reasoning that had brought him to the memory. First his name and the basic facts pertaining to himself, then the realization of where he was and the problem of why he happened to be there and finally the realization that he had a gun and that it was meant to be used. It was a logical way to think, a primer schoolbook way to work it out:

I am a man named Henderson James.

I live in a house on Summit Avenue.

Am I in the house on Summit Avenue?

No. I am not in the house on Summit Avenue.

I am on an embankment somewhere.

Why am I on the embankment?

But it wasn't the way a man thought, at least not the normal way a normal man would think. Man thought in shortcuts. He cut across the block and did not go all the way around.

It was a frightening thing, he told himself, this clear-around-the-block thinking. It wasn't normal and it wasn't right and it made no sense at all . . . no more sense than did the fact that he should find himself in a place with no memory of getting there.

He rose to his feet and ran his hands up and down his body. His clothes were neat, not rumpled. He hadn't been beaten up and he hadn't been thrown from a speeding car. There were no sore places on his body and his face was unbloody and whole and he felt all right.

He hooked his fingers in the holster belt and shucked it up so that it rode tightly on his hips. He pulled out the gun and checked it with expert and familiar fingers and the gun was ready.

He walked up the embankment and reached the road, went

across it with a swinging stride to reach the sidewalk that fronted the row of new bungalows. He heard a car coming and stepped off the sidewalk to crouch in a clump of evergreens that land-scaped one corner of the lawn. The move was instinctive and he crouched there, feeling just a little foolish at the thing he'd done.

The car went past and no one saw him. They would not, he now realized, have noticed him even if he had remained on the sidewalk.

He was unsure of himself; that must be the reason for his fear. There was a blank spot in his life, some mysterious incident that he did not know and the unknowing of it had undermined the sure and solid foundation of his own existence, had wrecked the basis of his motive and had turned him, momentarily, into a furtive animal that darted and hid at the approach of his fellow men.

That and something that had happened to him that made him think clear around the block.

He remained crouching in the evergreens, watching the street and the stretch of sidewalk, conscious of the white-painted, ghostly bungalows squatting back in their landscaped lots.

A word came into his mind. *Puudly.* An odd word, unearthly, yet it held terror.

The *puudly* had escaped and that was why he was here, hiding on the front lawn of some unsuspecting and sleeping citizen, equipped with a gun and a determination to use it, ready to match his wits and the quickness of brain and muscle against the most bloodthirsty, hate-filled thing yet found in the Galaxy.

The *puudly* was dangerous. It was not a thing to harbor. In fact, there was a law against harboring not only a *puudly*, but certain other alien beastlies even less lethal than a *puudly*. There was good reason for such a law, reason which no one, much less himself, would ever think to question.

And now the *puudly* was loose and somewhere in the city.

James grew cold at the thought of it, his brain forming images of the things that might come to pass if he did not hunt down the alien beast and put an end to it.

Although beast was not quite the word to use. The *puudly* was more than a beast . . . just how much more than a beast he once had hoped to learn. He had not learned a lot, he now admitted to himself, not nearly all there was to learn, but he had learned enough. More than enough to frighten him.

For one thing, he had learned what hate could be and how shallow an emotion human hate turned out when measured against the depth and intensity and the ravening horror of the *puudly*'s hate. Not unreasoning hate, for unreasoning hate defeats itself, but a rational, calculating, driving hate that motivated a clever and deadly killing maching which directed its rapacity and its cunning against every living thing that was not a *puudly*.

For the beast had a mind and a personality that operated upon the basic law of self-preservation against all comers, whoever they might be, extending that law to the interpretation that safety lay in one direction only . . . the death of every other living being. No other reason was needed for a *puudly*'s killing. The fact that anything else lived and moved and was thus posing a threat, no matter how remote, against a *puudly*, was sufficient reason in itself.

It was psychotic, of course, some murderous instinct planted far back in time and deep in the creature's racial consciousness, but no more psychotic, perhaps, than many human instincts.

The *puudly* had been, and still was, for that matter, a unique opportunity for a study in alien behaviorism. Given a permit, one could have studied them on their native planet. Refused a permit, one sometimes did a foolish thing, as James had.

And foolish acts backfire, as this one had.

James put down a hand and patted the gun at his side, as if by doing so he might derive some assurance that he was equal to the task. There was no question in his mind as to the thing that must be done. He must find the *puudly* and kill it and he must do that before the break of dawn. Anything less than that would be abject and horrifying failure.

For the *puudly* would bud. It was long past its time for the reproductive act and there were bare hours left to find it before it had loosed upon the Earth dozens of baby *puudlies*. They would not remain babies for long. A few hours after budding they would strike out on their own. To find one *puudly*, lost in the vastness of a sleeping city, seemed bad enough; to track down some dozens of them would be impossible.

So it was tonight or never.

Tonight there would be no killing on the *puudly*'s part. Tonight the beast would be intent on one thing only, to find a place where it could rest in quiet, where it could give itself over, wholeheartedly and with no interference, to the business of bringing other *puudlies* into being.

It was clever. It would have known where it was going before it had escaped. There would be, on its part, no time wasted in seeking or in doubling back. It would have known where it was going and already it was there, already the buds would be rising on its body, bursting forth and growing.

There was one place, and one place only, in the entire city where an alien beast would be safe from prying eyes. A man could figure that out and so could a *puudly*. The question was: Would the *puudly* know that man could figure it out? Would the *puudly* underestimate a man? Or, knowing that the man would know it, too, would it find another place of hiding?

James rose from the evergreens and went down the sidewalk. The street marker at the corner, standing underneath a swinging street light, told him where he was and it was closer to the place where he was going than he might have hoped.

II

The zoo was quiet for a while, and then something sent up a howl that raised James's hackles and made his blood stop in his veins.

James, having scaled the fence, stood tensely at its foot, trying to identify the howling animal. He was unable to place it. More than likely, he told himself, it was a new one. A person simply couldn't keep track of all the zoo's occupants. New ones were coming in all the time, strange, unheard-of creatures from the distant stars.

Straight ahead lay the unoccupied moat cage that up until a day or two before had held an unbelievable monstrosity from the jungles of one of the Arctian worlds. James grimaced in the dark, remembering the thing. They had finally had to kill it.

And now the *puudly* was there . . . well, maybe not there, but one place that it could be, the one place in the entire city where it might be seen and arouse no comment, for the zoo was filled with animals that were seldom seen and another strange one would arouse only momentary wonder. One animal more would go unnoticed unless some zoo attendant should think to check the records.

There, in that unoccupied cage area, the *puudly* would be undisturbed, could go quietly about its business of budding out more *puudlies*. No one would bother it, for things like *puudlies* were the normal occupants of this place set aside for the strangers brought to Earth to be stared at and studied by that ferocious race, the humans.

James stood quietly beside the fence.

Henderson James. Thirty-six. Unmarried. Alien psychologist. An official of this zoo. And an offender against the law for having secured and harbored an alien being that was barred from Earth.

Why, he asked himself, did he think of himself in this way? Why, standing here, did he catalogue himself? It was instinctive to know one's self . . . there was no need, no sense of setting up a mental outline of one's self.

It had been foolish to go ahead with this *puudly* business. He recalled now how he had spent days fighting it out with himself, reviewing all the disastrous possibilities which might arise from it. If the old renegade spaceman had not come to him and had not said, over a bottle of most delicious Lupan wine, that he could deliver, for a certain rather staggering sum, one live *puudly*, in good condition, it would never have happened.

James was sure that of himself he never would have thought of it. But the old space captain was a man he knew and admired from former dealings. He was a man who was not averse to turning either an honest or a dishonest dollar, and yet he was a man, for all of that, you could depend upon. He would do what you paid him for and keep his lip buttoned tight once the deed was done.

James had wanted a *puudly*, for it was a most engaging beast with certain little tricks that, once understood, might open up new avenues of speculation and approach, might write new chapters in the tortuous study of alien minds and manners.

But for all of that, it had been a terrifying thing to do and now that the beast was loose, the terror was compounded. For it was not wholly beyond speculation that the descendants of this one brood that the escaped *puudly* would spawn might wipe out the population of the Earth, or at best, make the Earth untenable for its rightful dwellers.

A place like the Earth, with its teeming millions, would provide a field day for the fangs of the *puudlies*, and the minds that drove the fangs. They would not hunt for hunger, nor for the sheer madness of the kill, but because of the compelling conviction that no *puudly* would be safe until Earth was wiped clean of life. They would be killing for survival, as a cornered rat would kill . . . except that they would be cornered nowhere but in the murderous insecurity of their minds.

If the posses scoured the Earth to hunt them down, they would be found in all directions, for they would be shrewd enough to scatter. They would know the ways of guns and traps and poisons and there would be more and more of them as time went on. Each of them would accelerate its budding to replace with a dozen or a hundred the ones that might be killed.

James moved quietly forward to the edge of the moat and let himself down into the mud that covered the bottom. When the monstrosity had been killed, the moat had been drained and should long since have been cleaned, but the press of work, James thought, must have prevented its getting done.

Slowly he waded out into the mud, feeling his way, his feet making sucking noises as he pulled them through the slime. Finally he reached the rocky incline that led out of the moat to the island cage.

He stood for a moment, his hands on the great, wet boulders, listening, trying to hold his breath so the sound of it would not interfere with his hearing. The thing that howled had quieted and the night was deathly quiet. Or seemed, at first, to be. Then he heard the little insect noises that ran through the grass and bushes and the whisper of the leaves in the trees across the moat and the far-off sound that was the hoarse breathing of a sleeping city.

Now, for the first time, he felt fear. Felt it in the silence that was not a silence, in the mud beneath his feet, in the upthrust boulders that rose out of the moat.

The *puudly* was a dangerous thing, not only because it was strong and quick, but because it was intelligent. Just how intelligent, he did not know. It reasoned and it planned and schemed. It could talk, though not as a human talks . . . probably better than a human ever could. For it could not only talk words, but it could talk emotions. It lured its victims to it by the thoughts it put into their minds; it held them entranced with dreams and illusion until it slit their throats. It could purr a man to sleep, could lull him to suicidal inaction. It could drive him crazy with a single flickering thought, hurling a perception so foul and alien that the mind recoiled deep inside itself and stayed there, coiled tight, like a watch that has been overwound and will not run.

It should have budded long ago, but it had fought off its budding, holding back against the day when it might escape, planning, he realized now, its fight to stay on Earth, which meant its conquest of Earth. It had planned, and planned well, against this very moment, and it would feel or show no mercy to anyone who interfered with it.

His hand went down and touched the gun and he felt the muscles in his jaw involuntarily tightening, and suddenly there was at once a lightness and a hardness in him that had not been there before. He pulled himself up the boulder face, seeking cautious hand- and toeholds, breathing shallowly, body pressed against the rock. Quickly, and surely, and no noise, for he must reach the top and be there before the *puudly* knew there was anyone around.

The *puudly* would be relaxed and intent upon its business, engrossed in the budding forth of that numerous family that in days to come would begin the grim and relentless crusade to make an alien planet safe for *puudlies* ... and for *puudlies* alone.

That is, if the *puudly* was here and not somewhere else. James was only a human trying to think like a *puudly* and that was not an easy or pleasant job and he had no way of knowing if he succeeded. He could only hope that his reasoning was vicious and crafty enough.

His clawing hand found grass and earth and he sank his fingers deep into the soil, hauling his body the last few feet of the rock face above the pit.

He lay flat upon the gently sloping ground, listening, tensed for any danger. He studied the ground in front of him, probing every foot. Distant street lamps lighting the zoo walks threw back the total blackness that had engulfed him as he climbed out of the moat, but there still were areas of shadow that he had to study closely.

Inch by inch, he squirmed his way along, making sure of the terrain immediately ahead before he moved a muscle. He held the gun in a rock-hard fist, ready for instant action, watching for the faintest hint of motion, alert for any hump or irregularity that was not rock or bush or grass.

Minutes magnified themselves into hours, his eyes ached with staring, and the lightness that had been in him drained away, leaving only the hardness, which was as tense as a drawn bowstring. A sense of failure began to seep into his mind and with it came the full-fledged, until now unadmitted, realization of what failure meant, not only for the world, but for the dignity and the pride that was Henderson James.

Now, faced with the possibility, he admitted to himself the action he must take if the *puudly* was not here, if he did not find it here and kill it. He would have to notify the authorities, would have to attempt to alert the police, must plead with the newspapers and radio to warn the citizenry, must reveal himself as a man who, through pride and self-conceit, had exposed the people of Earth to this threat against their hold upon their native planet.

They would not believe him. They would laugh at him until the laughter died in their torn throats, choked off with their blood. He sweated, thinking of it, thinking of the price this city, and the world, would pay before it learned the truth.

There was a whisper of sound, a movement of black against deeper black.

The *puudly* rose in front of him, not more than six feet away, from its bed beside a bush. He jerked the pistol up and his finger tightened on the trigger.

"Don't," the *puudly* said inside his mind. "I'll go along with you."

His finger strained with the careful slowness of the squeeze and the gun leaped in his hand, but even as it did he felt the whiplash of terror slash at his brain, caught for just a second the terrible import, the mind-shattering obscenity that glanced off his mind and ricocheted away.

"Too late," he told the *puudly*, with his voice and his mind and his body shaking. "You should have tried that first. You wasted precious seconds. You would have got me if you had done it first."

It had been easy, he assured himself, much easier that he had thought. The *puudly* was dead or dying and the Earth and its millions of unsuspecting citizens were safe, and, best of all, Henderson James was safe . . . safe from indignity, safe from being stripped naked of the little defenses he had built up through the years to shield him against the public stare. He felt relief flood over him and it left him pulseless and breathless and feeling clean, but weak.

"You fool," the dying *puudly* said, death clouding its words as they built up in his mind. "You fool, you half-thing, you duplicate. . . ."

It died then and he felt it die, felt the life go out of it and leave it empty.

He rose softly to his feet and he seemed stunned and at first he thought it was from knowing death, from having touched hands with death within the *puudly's* mind.

The *puudly* had tried to fool him. Faced with the pistol, it had tried to throw him off his balance to give it the second that it needed to hurl the mind-blasting thought that had caught at the edge of his brain. If he had hesitated for a moment, he knew, it would have been all over with him. If his finger had slackened for a moment, it would have been too late.

The *puudly* must have known that he would think of the zoo as the first logical place to look and, even knowing that, it had held him in enough contempt to come here, had not even bothered to try to watch for him, had not tried to stalk him, had waited until he was almost on top of it before it moved.

And that was queer, for the *puudly* must have known, with its uncanny mental powers, every move that he had made. It must have maintained a casual contact with his mind every second of the time since it had escaped. He had known that and . . . wait a minute, he hadn't known it until this very moment, although, knowing it now, it seemed as if he had always known it.

What is the matter with me? he thought. There's something wrong with me. I should have known I could not surprise the *puudly*, and yet I didn't know it. I must have surprised it, for otherwise it would have finished me off quite leisurely at any moment after I climbed out of the moat.

You fool, the *puudly* had said. You fool, you half-thing, you duplicate. . . .

You duplicate!

He felt the strength and the personality and the hard, un-questioned identity of himself as Henderson James, human being, drain out of him as if someone had cut the puppet string and he, the puppet, had slumped supine upon the stage.

So that was why he was able to surprise the *puudly*!

There were two Henderson Jameses. The *puudly* had been in contact with one of them, the original, the real Henderson James, had known every move he made, had known that it was safe so far as Henderson James might be concerned. It had not known of the second Henderson James who had stalked it through the night.

Henderson James, duplicate.

Henderson James, temporary.

Henderson James, here tonight, gone tomorrow.

For they would not let him live. The original Henderson James would not allow him to continue living, and even if he did, the world would not allow it. Duplicates were made only for very temporary and very special reasons, and it was always understood that once their purpose was accomplished they would be done away with.

Done away with . . . those were the words exactly. Gotten out of the way. Swept out of sight and mind. Killed as unconcernedly and emotionlessly as one chops off a chicken's head.

He walked forward and dropped on one knee beside the *puudly*, running his hand over its body in the darkness. Lumps stood out all over it, the swelling buds that now would never break to spew forth in a loathsome birth of a brood of *puudly* pups.

He rose to his feet.

The job was done. The *puudly* had been killed—killed before it had given birth to a horde of horrors.

The job was done and he could go home.

Home?

Of course, that was the thing that had been planted in his mind, the thing they wanted him to do. To go home, to go back to the house on Summit Avenue, where his executioners would wait, to walk back deliberately and unsuspectingly to the death that waited.

The job was done and his usefulness was over. He had been created to perform a certain task and the task was now performed and while an hour ago he had been a factor in the plans of men, he was no longer wanted. He was an embarrassment and superfluous.

Now wait a minute, he told himself. You may not be a duplicate. You do not feel like one.

That was true. He felt like Henderson James. He was Henderson James. He lived on Summit Avenue and had illegally brought to Earth a beast known as a *puudly* in order that he might study it and talk to it and test its alien reactions, attempt to measure its intelligence and guess at the strength and depth and the direction of its non-humanity. He had been a fool, of course, to do it, and yet at the time it had seemed important to understand the deadly, alien mentality.

I am a human, he said, and that was right, but even so the fact meant nothing. Of course he was human. Henderson James was human and his duplicate would be exactly as human as the original. For the duplicate, processed from the pattern that held every trait and characteristic of the man he was to become a copy of, would differ in not a single basic factor.

In not a single basic factor, perhaps, but in other things. For no matter how much the duplicate might be like his pattern, no matter how full-limbed he might spring from his creation, he still would be a new man. He would have the capacity for knowledge and for thought and in a little time he would have and know and be all the things that his original was. . . .

But it would take some time, some short while to come to a full realization of all he knew and was, some time to coordinate and recognize all the knowledge and experience that lay within his mind. At first he'd grope and search until he came upon the things that he must know. Until he became acquainted with himself, with the sort of man he was, he could not reach out blindly in the dark and put his hand exactly and unerringly upon the thing he wished.

That had been exactly what he'd done. He had groped and searched. He had been compelled to think, at first, in simple basic truths and facts.

I am a man.

I am on a planet called Earth.

I am Henderson James.

I live on Summit Avenue.

There is a job to do.

It had been quite a while, he remembered now, before he had been able to dig out of his mind the nature of the job.

There is a *puudly* to hunt down and destroy.

Even now he could not find in the hidden, still-veiled recesses of his mind the many valid reasons why a man should run so grave a risk to study a thing so vicious as a *puudly*. There were reasons, he knew there were, and in a little time he would know them quite specifically.

The point was that if he were Henderson James, original, he would know them now, know them as a part of himself and his life, without laboriously searching for them.

The *puudly* had known, of course. It had known, beyond any chance of error, that there were two Henderson Jameses. It had been keeping tab on one when another one showed up. A mentality far less astute than the *puudly's* would have had no trouble in figuring that one out.

If the *puudly* had not talked, he told himself, I never would have known. If he had died at once and not had a chance to taunt me, I would not have known, I would even now be walking to the house on Summit Avenue.

He stood lonely and naked of soul in the wind that swept across the moated island. There was a sour bitterness in his mouth.

He moved a foot and touched the dead *puudly*.

"I'm sorry," he told the stiffening body. "I'm sorry now I did it. If I had known, I never would have killed you."

Stiffly erect, he moved away.

III

He stopped at the street corner, keeping well in the shadow. Halfway down the block, and on the other side, was the house. A light burned in one of the rooms upstairs and another on the post beside the gate that opened into the yard, lighting the walk up to the door.

Just as if, he told himself, the house were waiting for the master to come home. And that, of course, was exactly what it was doing. An old lady of a house, waiting, hands folded in its lap, rocking very gently in a squeaky chair . . . and with a gun beneath the folded shawl.

His lip lifted in half a snarl as he stood there, looking at the house. What do they take me for? he thought, putting out a trap in plain sight and one that's not even baited? Then he remembered. They would not know, of course, that he knew he was a duplicate. They would think that he would think that he was Henderson James, the one and only. They would expect him to come walking home, quite naturally, believing he belonged there. So far as they would know, there would be no possibility of his finding out the truth.

And now that he had? Now that he was here, across the street from the waiting house?

He had been brought into being, had been given life, to do a job that his original had not dared to do, or had not wanted to do. He had carried out a killing his original didn't want to dirty his hands with, or risk his neck in doing.

Or had it not been that at all, but the necessity of two men working on the job, the original serving as a focus for the *puudly's* watchful mind while the other man sneaked up to kill it while it watched?

No matter what, he had been created, at a good stiff price, from the pattern of the man that was Henderson James. The wizardry of man's knowledge, the magic of machines, a deep understanding of organic chemistry, of human physiology, of the mystery of life, had made a second Henderson James. It was legal, of course, under certain circumstances . . . for example, in the case of public policy, and his own creation, he knew, might have been validated under such a heading. But there were conditions, and one of these was that a duplicate not be allowed to continue living once it had served the specific purpose for which it had been created.

Usually such a condition was a simple one to carry out, for the duplicate was not meant to know he was a duplicate. So far as he was concerned, he was the original. There was no suspicion in him, no foreknowledge of the doom that was inevitably ordered for him, no reason for him to be on guard against the death that waited.

The duplicate knitted his brow, trying to puzzle it out.

There was a strange set of ethics here.

He was alive and he wanted to stay alive. Life, once it had been tasted, was too sweet, too good, to go back to the nothingness from which he had come . . . or would it be nothingness? Now that he had known life, now that he was alive, might he not hope for a life after death, the same as any other human being? Might not he, too, have the same human right as any other human to grasp at the shadowy and glorious promises and assurances held out by religion and by faith?

He tried to marshall what he knew about those promises and assurances, but his knowledge was illusive. A little later he would remember more about it. A little later, when the neural bookkeeper in his mind had been able to coordinate and activate the knowledge that he had inherited from his pattern, he would know.

He felt a trace of anger stir deep inside him, anger at the unfairness of allowing him only a few short hours of life, of allowing to learn how wonderful a thing life was, only to snatch it from him. It was a cruelty that went beyond mere human cruelty. It was something that had been fashioned out of the distorted perspective of a machine society that measured existence only in terms of mechanical and physical worth, that discarded with a ruthless hand whatever part of society that had no specific purpose.

The cruelty, he told himself, was in ever giving life, not in taking it away.

His original, of course, was the one to blame. He was the one who had obtained the *puudly* and allowed it to escape. It was his fumbling and his inability to correct his error without help which had created the necessity of fashioning a duplicate.

And yet, could he blame him?

Perhaps, rather, he owed him gratitude for a few hours of life at least, gratitude for the privilege of knowing what life was like. Although he could not quite decide whether or not it was something which called for gratitude.

He stood there, staring at the house. That light in the upstairs room was in the study of the master bedroom. Up there Henderson James, original, was waiting for the word that the duplicate had come home to death. It was an easy thing to sit there and wait, to sit and wait for the word that was sure to come. An easy thing to sentence to death a man one had never seen, even if that man be the walking image of one's self.

It would be a harder decision to kill him if you stood face to face with him . . . harder to kill someone who would be, of necessity, closer than a brother, someone who would be, even literally, flesh of your flesh, blood of your blood, brain of your brain.

There would be a practical side as well, a great advantage to be able to work with a man who thought as you did, who would be almost a second self. It would be almost as if there were two of you.

A thing like that could be arranged. Plastic surgery and a price for secrecy could make your duplicate into an unrecognizable other person. A little red tape, some finagling . . . but it could be done. It was a proposition Henderson James, duplicate, thought would interest Henderson James, original. Or at least he hoped it would.

The room with the light could be reached with a little luck, with strength and agility and determination. The brick expanse of a chimney, its base cloaked by shrubs, its length masked by a closely growing tree, ran up the wall. A man could climb its rough brick face, could reach out and swing himself through the open window into the lighted room.

And once Henderson James, original, stood face to face with Henderson James, duplicate . . . well, it would be less of a gamble. The duplicate than would no longer be an impersonal factor. He would be a man and one that was very close to his original.

There would be watchers, but they would be watching the front door. If he was quiet, if he could reach and climb the chimney without making any noise, he'd be in the room before anyone would notice.

He drew back deeper in the shadows and considered. It was either get into the room and face his original, hope to be able to strike a compromise with him, or simply to light out . . . to run and hide and wait, watching his chance to get completely away, perhaps to some far planet in some other part of the Galaxy.

Both ways were a gamble, but one was quick, would either succeed or fail within the hour; the other might drag on for months, with a man never knowing whether he was safe, never being sure.

Something nagged at him, a persistent little fact that skittered through his brain and eluded his efforts to pin it down. It might be important and then, again, it might be a random thing, simply a floating piece of information that was looking for its pigeonhole.

His mind shrugged it off.

The quick way or the long way?

He stood thinking for a moment and then moved swiftly down

the street, seeking a place where he could cross in shadow.

He had chosen the short way.

IV

The room was empty.

He stood beside the window, quietly, only his eyes moving, searching every corner, checking against a situation that couldn't seem quite true . . . that Henderson James was not here, waiting for the word.

Then he strode swiftly to the bedroom door and swung it open. His finger found the switch and the lights went on. The bedroom was empty and so was the bath. He went back into the study.

He stood with his back against the wall, facing the door that led into the hallway, but his eyes went over the room, foot by foot, orienting himself, feeling himself flow into the shape and form of it, feeling familiarity creep in upon him and enfold him in its comfort of belonging.

Here were the books, the fireplace with its mantel loaded with souvenirs, the easy chairs, the liquor cabinet . . . and all were a part of him, a background that was as much a part of Henderson James as his body and his inner thoughts were a part of him.

This, he thought, is what I would have missed, the experience I never would have had if the *puudly* had not taunted me. I would have died an empty and unrelated body that had no actual place in the universe.

The phone purred at him and he stood there startled by it, as if some intruder from the outside had pushed its way into the room, shattering the sense of belonging that had come to him.

The phone rang again and he went across the room and picked it up.

"James speaking," he said.

"That you, Mr. James?"

The voice was that of Anderson, the gardener.

"Why, yes," said the duplicate. "Who did you think it was?"

"We got a fellow here who says he's you."

Henderson James, duplicate, stiffened with fright and his hand, suddenly, was grasping the phone so hard that he found the time to wonder why it did not pulverize to bits beneath his fingers.

"He's dressed like you," the gardener said, "and I knew you went out. Talked to you, remember? Told you that you shouldn't? Not with us waiting for that . . . that thing."

"Yes," said the duplicate, his voice so even that he could not believe it was he who spoke. "Yes, certainly I remember talking with you."

"But, sir, how did you get back?"

"I came in the back way," the even voice said into the phone. "Now what's holding you back?"

"He's dressed like you."

"Naturally. Of course he would be, Anderson."

And that, to be sure, didn't quite follow, but Anderson wasn't too bright to start with and now he was somewhat upset.

"You remember," the duplicate said, "that we talked about it."

"I guess I was excited and forgot," admitted Anderson. "You told me to call you, to make sure you were in your study, though. That's right, isn't it, sir?"

"You've called me," the duplicate said, "and I am here."

"Then the other one out here is him?"

"Of course," said the duplicate. "Who else could it be?"

He put the phone back into the cradle and stood waiting. It came a moment after, the dull, throaty cough of a gun.

He walked to a chair and sank into it, spent with the knowledge of how events had been so ordered that now, finally, he was safe, safe beyond all question.

Soon he would have to change into other clothes, hide the gun and the clothes that he was wearing. The staff would ask no questions, most likely, but it was best to let nothing arouse suspicion in their minds.

He felt his nerves quieting and he allowed himself to glance about the room, take in the books and furnishings, the soft and easy . . . and earned . . . comfort of a man solidly and unshakably established in the world.

He smiled softly.

"It will be nice," he said.

It had been easy. Now it was over, it seemed ridiculously easy. Easy because he had never seen the man who had walked up to the door. It was easy to kill a man you have never seen.

With each passing hour he would slip deeper and deeper into the personality that was his by right of heritage. There would be no one to question, after a time not even himself, that he was Henderson James.

The phone rang again and he got up to answer it.

A pleasant voice told him, "This is Allen, over at the duplication lab. We've been waiting for a report from you."

"Well," said James, "I . . ."

"I just called," interrupted Allen, "to tell you not to worry. It slipped my mind before."

"I see," said James, though he didn't.

"We did this one a little differently," Allen explained. "An experiment that we thought we'd try out. Slow poison in his bloodstream. Just another precaution. Probably not necessary, but we like to be positive. In case he fails to show up, you needn't worry any."

"I am sure he will show up."

Allen chuckled. "Twenty-four hours. Like a time bomb. No antidote for it even if he found out somehow."

"It was good of you to let me know," said James.

"Glad to," said Allen. "Good night, Mr. James."

EVIDENCE

Isaac Asimov

Isaac Asimov's classic book I, Robot *gave us the elegantly logical Three Laws of Robotics that will almost certainly govern the relationship between humans and their mechanical servants when robots become commonplace home appliances. To find one of Asimov's robot stories in this collection may seem surprising, for his subject is not androids at all, but true machines. However, there* is *an exception—a story about a being that might just be an android robot. . . .*

Francis Quinn was a politician of the new school. That, of course, is a meaningless expression, as are all expressions of the sort. Most of the "new schools" we have were duplicated in the social life of ancient Greece, and perhaps, if we knew more about it, in the social life of ancient Sumeria and in the lake dwellings of prehistoric Switzerland as well.

But, to get out from under what promises to be a dull and complicated beginning, it might be best to state hastily that Quinn neither ran for office nor canvassed for votes, made no speeches and stuffed no ballot boxes. Any more than Napoleon pulled a trigger at Austerlitz.

And since politics makes strange bedfellows, Alfred Lanning sat at the other side of the desk with his ferocious white eyebrows bent far forward over eyes in which chronic impatience had sharpened to acuity. He was not pleased.

The fact, if known to Quinn, would have annoyed him not the least. His voice was friendly, perhaps professionally so.

"I assume you know Stephen Byerly, Dr. Lanning."

"I have heard of him. So have many people."

"Yes, so have I. Perhaps you intend voting for him in the next election."

"I couldn't say." There was an unmistakable trace of acidity here. "I have not followed the political currents, so I'm not aware that he is running for office."

"He may be our next mayor. Of course, he is only a lawyer now, but great oaks—"

"Yes," interrupted Lanning, "I have heard the phrase before. But I wonder if we can get to the business at hand."

"We *are* at the business at hand, Dr. Lanning." Quinn's tone was very gentle, "It is to my interest to keep Mr. Byerly a district attorney at the very most, and it is to your interest to help me do so."

"To *my* interest? Come!" Lanning's eyebrows hunched low.

"Well, say then to the interest of the U.S. Robots and Mechanical Men Corporation. I come to you as Director-Emeritus of Research, because I know that your connection to them is that of, shall we say, 'elder statesman.' You are listened to with respect and yet your connection with them is no longer so tight but that you cannot possess considerable freedom of action; even if the action is somewhat unorthodox."

Dr. Lanning was silent a moment, chewing the cud of his thoughts. He said more softly, "I don't follow you at all, Mr. Quinn."

"I am not surprised, Dr. Lanning. But it's all rather simple.

Do you mind?'' Quinn lit a slender cigarette with a lighter of tasteful simplicity and his big-boned face settled into an expression of quiet amusement. "We have spoken of Mr. Byerly—a strange and colorful character. He was unknown three years ago. He is very well known now. He is a man of force and ability, and certainly the most capable and intelligent prosecutor I have ever known. Unfortunately he is not a friend of mine—''

"I understand," said Lanning, mechanically. He stared at his fingernails.

"I have had occasion," continued Quinn, evenly, "in the past year to investigate Mr. Byerly—quite exhaustively. It is always useful, you see, to subject the past life of reform politicians to rather inquisitive search. If you knew how often it helped—'' He paused to smile humorlessly at the glowing tip of his cigarette. "But Mr. Byerly's past is unremarkable. A quiet life in a small town, a college education, a wife who died young, an auto accident with a slow recovery, law school, coming to the metropolis, an attorney."

Francis Quinn shook his head slowly, then added, "But his present life. Ah, that is remarkable. Our district attorney never eats!''

Lanning's head snapped up, old eyes surprisingly sharp, "Pardon me?''

"Our district attorney never eats." The repetition thumped by syllables. "I'll modify that slightly. He has never been seen to eat or drink. Never! Do you understand the significance of the word? Not rarely, but never!''

"I find that quite incredible. Can you trust your investigators?''

"I can trust my investigators, and I don't find it incredible at all. Further, our district attorney has never been seen to drink—in the aqueous sense as well as the alcoholic—nor to sleep.

There are other factors, but I should think I have made my point.''

Lanning leaned back in his seat, and there was the rapt silence of challenge and response between them, and then the old roboticist shook his head. ''No. There is only one thing you can be trying to imply, if I couple your statements with the fact that you present them to me, and that is impossible.''

''But the man is quite inhuman, Dr. Lanning.''

''If you told me he were Satan in masquerade, there would be a faint chance that I might believe you.''

''I tell you he is a robot, Dr. Lanning.''

''I tell you it is as impossible a conception as I have ever heard, Mr. Quinn.''

Again the combative silence.

''Nevertheless,'' and Quinn stubbed out his cigarette with elaborate care, ''you will have to investigate this impossibility with all the resources of the Corporation.''

''I'm sure I could undertake no such thing, Mr. Quinn. You don't seriously suggest that the Corporation take part in local politics.''

''You have no choice. Supposing I were to make my facts public without proof. The evidence is circumstantial enough.''

''Suit yourself in that respect.''

''But it would not suit me. Proof would be much preferable. And it would not suit *you*, for the publicity would be very damaging to your company. You are perfectly well acquainted, I suppose, with the strict rules against the use of robots on inhabited worlds.''

''Certainly!''—brusquely.

''You know that the U.S. Robot and Mechanical Men Corporation is the only manufacturer of positronic robots in the Solar System, and if Byerly is a robot, he is a *positronic* robot. You are also aware that all positronic robots are leased, and not sold;

that the corporation remains the owner and manager of each robot, and is therefore responsible for the actions of all."

"It is an easy matter, Mr. Quinn, to prove the corporation has never manufactured a robot of humanoid character."

"It can be done? To discuss merely possibilities."

"Yes. It can be done."

"Secretly, I imagine, as well. Without entering it in your books."

"Not the positronic brain, sir. Too many factors are involved in that, and there is the tightest possible government supervision."

"Yes, but robots are worn out, break down, go out of order— and are dismantled."

"And the positronic brains re-used or destroyed."

"Really?" Francis Quinn allowed himself a trace of sarcasm. "And if one were, accidentally, of course, not destroyed—and there happened to be a humanoid structure waiting for a brain."

"Impossible!"

"You would have to prove that to the government and the public, so why not prove it to me now."

"But what could our purpose be?" demanded Lanning in exasperation. "Where is our motivation? Credit us with a minimum of sense."

"My dear sir, please. The Corporation would be only too glad to have the various Regions permit the use of humanoid positronic robots on inhabited worlds. The profits would be enormous. But the prejudice of public against such a practice is too great. Suppose you get them used to such robots first—see, we have a skillful lawyer, a good mayor—and he is a robot. Won't you buy our robot butlers?"

"Thoroughly fantastic. An almost humorous descent to the ridiculous."

"I imagine so. Why not prove it? Or would you still rather try to prove it to the public?"

The light in the office was dimming, but it was not yet too dim to obscure the flush of frustration on Alfred Lanning's face. Slowly, the roboticist's finger touched a knob and the wall illuminators glowed to gentle life.

"Well, then," he growled, "let us see."

The face of Stephen Byerly is not an easy one to describe. He was forty by birth certificate and forty by appearance—but it was a healthy, well-nourished good-natured appearance of forty; one that automatically drew the teeth of the bromide about "looking one's age."

This was particularly true when he laughed, and he was laughing now. It came loudly and continuously, died away for a bit, then began again—

And Alfred Lanning's face contracted into a rigidly bitter monument of disapproval. He made a half gesture to the woman who sat beside him, but her thin, bloodless lips merely pursed themselves a trifle.

Byerly gasped himself a stage nearer normality.

"Really, Dr. Lanning . . . really—I . . . *I* . . . a robot?"

Lanning bit his words off with a snap, "It is no statement of mine, sir. I would be quite satisfied to have you a member of humanity. Since our corporation never manufactured you, I am quite certain that you are—in a legalistic sense, at any rate. But since the contention that you are a robot has been advanced to us seriously by a man of certain standing—"

"Don't mention his name, if it would knock a chip off your granite block of ethics, but let's pretend it was Frank Quinn, for the sake of argument, and continue."

Lanning drew in a sharp, cutting snort at the interruption, and paused ferociously before continuing with added frigidity, "—by a man of certain standing, with whose identity I am not interested in playing guessing games, I am bound to ask your co-operation in disproving it. The mere fact that such a contention could be advanced and publicized by the means at this man's disposal would be a bad blow to the company I represent—even if the charge were never proven. You understand me?''

''Oh, yes, your position is clear to me. The charge itself is ridiculous. The spot you find yourself in is not. I beg your pardon, if my laughter offended you. It was the first I laughed at, not the second. How can I help you?''

''It could be very simple. you have only to sit down to a meal at a restaurant in the presence of witnesses, have your picture taken, and eat.'' Lanning sat back in his chair, the worst of the interview over. The woman beside him watched Byerly with an apparently absorbed expression but contributed nothing of her own.

Stephen Byerly met her eyes for an instant, was caught by them, then turned back to the roboticist. For a while his fingers were thoughtful over the bronze paperweight that was the only ornament on his desk.

He said quietly, ''I don't think I can oblige you.''

He raised his hand. ''Now wait, Dr. Lanning. I appreciate the fact that this whole matter is distasteful to you, that you have been forced into it against your will, that you feel you are playing an undignified and even ridiculous part. Still, the matter is even more intimately concerned with myself, so be tolerant.

''First, what makes you think that Quinn—this man of certain standing, you know—wasn't hoodwinking you, in order to get you to do exactly what you are doing?''

''Why, it seems scarcely likely that a reputable person would endanger himself in so ridiculous a fashion, if he weren't convinced he was on safe ground.''

There was little humor in Byerly's eyes. ''You don't know Quinn. He could manage to make safe ground out of a ledge a mountain sheep could not handle. I suppose he showed the particulars of the investigation he claims to have made of me?''

"Enough to convince me that it would be too troublesome to have our corporation attempt to disprove them when you could do so more easily."

"Then you believe him when he says I never eat. You are a scientist, Dr. Lanning. Think of the logic required. I have not been observed to eat, therefore, I never eat. Q.E.D. After all!"

"You are using prosecution tactics to confuse what is really a very simple situation."

"On the contrary, I am trying to clarify what you and Quinn between you are making a very complicated one. You see, I don't sleep much, that's true, and I certainly don't sleep in public. I have never cared to eat with others—an idiosyncracy which is unusual and probably neurotic in character, but which harms no one. Look, Dr. Lanning, let me present you with a suppositious case. Supposing we had a politician who was interested in defeating a reform candidate at any cost and while investigating his private life came across oddities such as I have just mentioned.

"Suppose further that in order to smear the candidate effectively, he comes to your company as the ideal agent. Do you expect him to say to you, 'So-and-so is a robot because he hardly ever eats with people, and I have never seen him fall asleep in the middle of a case; and once when I peeped into his window in the middle of the night, there he was, sitting up with a book; and I looked in his frigidaire and there was no food in it.'

"If he told you that, you would send for a straitjacket. But if he tells you, 'he *never* sleeps; he *never* eats,' then the shock of the statement blinds you to the fact that such statements are impossible to prove. You play into his hands by contributing to the to-do."

"Regardless, sir," began Lanning, with a threatening obstinacy, "of whether you consider this matter serious or not, it will require only the meal I mentioned to end it."

Again Byerly turned to the woman, who still regarded him

expressionlessly. "Pardon me. I've caught your name correctly, haven't I? Dr. Susan Calvin?"

"Yes, Mr. Byerly."

"You're the U.S. Robot's psychologist, aren't you?"

"*Robo*psychologist, please."

"Oh, are robots so different from men, mentally?"

"Worlds different." She allowed herself a frosty smile. "Robots are essentially decent."

Humor tugged the corners of the lawyer's mouth. "Well, that's a hard blow. But what I wanted to say was this. Since you're a psycho—a robopsychologist, *and* a woman, I'll bet you've thought of something that Dr. Lanning hasn't thought of."

"And what is that?"

"You've got something to eat in your purse."

Something caught the schooled indifference of Susan Calvin's eyes. She said, "You surprise me, Mr. Byerly."

And opening her purse, she produced an apple. Quietly, she handed it to him. Dr. Lanning, after an initial start, followed the slow movement from one hand to the other with sharply alert eyes.

Calmly, Stephen Byerly bit into it, and calmly he swallowed it.

"You see, Dr. Lanning?"

Dr. Lanning smiled in a relief tangible enough to make even his eyebrows appear benevolent. A relief that survived for one fragile second.

Susan Calvin said, "I was curious to see if you would eat it, but, of course, in the present case, it proves nothing."

Byerly grinned. "It doesn't?"

"Of course not. It is obvious, Dr. Lanning, that if this man were a humanoid robot, he would be a perfect imitation. He is almost too human to be credible. After all, we have been seeing and observing human beings all our lives; it would be impossible to palm something merely nearly right off on us. It would have to be *all* right. Observe the texture of the skin, the quality of the irises, the bone formation of the hand. If he's a robot, I wish U.S. Robots *had* made him, because he's a good job. Do you suppose then, that anyone capable of paying attention to such niceties would neglect a few gadgets to take care of such things as eating, sleeping, elimination? For emergency use only, perhaps; as, for instance, to prevent such situations as are arising here. So a meal won't really prove anything."

"Now wait," snarled Lanning. "I am not quite the fool both of you make me out to be. I am not interested in the problem of Mr. Byerly's humanity or nonhumanity. I am interested in getting the corporation out of a hole. A public meal will end the matter and keep it ended no matter what Quinn does. We can leave the finer details to lawyers and robopsychologists."

"But, Dr. Lanning," said Byerly, "you forget the politics of the situation. I am as anxious to be elected as Quinn is to stop me. By the way, did you notice that you used his name? It's a cheap shyster trick of mine; I knew you would, before you were through."

Lanning flushed, "What has the election to do with it?"

"Publicity works both ways, sir. If Quinn wants to call me a robot, and has the nerve to do so, I have the nerve to play the game his way."

"You mean you—" Lanning was quite frankly appalled.

"Exactly. I mean that I'm going to let him go ahead, choose his rope, test its strength, cut off the right length, tie the noose, insert his head and grin. I can do what little else is required."

"You are mighty confident."

Susan Calvin rose to her feet. "Come, Alfred, we won't change his mind for him."

"You see." Byerly smiled gently. "You're a human psychologist, too."

But perhaps not all the confidence that Dr. Lanning had remarked upon was present that evening when Byerly's car parked on the automatic treads leading to the sunken garage, and Byerly himself crossed the path to the front door of his house.

The figure in the wheelchair looked up as he entered and smiled. Byerly's face lit with affection. He crossed over to it.

The cripple's voice was a hoarse, grating whisper that came out of a mouth forever twisted to one side, leering out of a face that was half scar tissue. "You're late, Steve."

"I know, John, I know. But I've been up against a peculiar and interesting trouble today."

"So?" Neither the torn face nor the destroyed voice could carry expression but there was anxiety in the clear eyes. "Nothing you can't handle?"

"I'm not exactly certain. I may need your help. *You're* the brilliant one in the family. Do you want me to take you out into the garden? It's a beautiful evening."

Two strong arms lifted John from the wheelchair. Gently, almost caressingly, Byerly's arms went around the shoulders and under the swathed legs of the cripple. Carefully, and slowly, he walked through the rooms, down the gentle ramp that had been built with a wheelchair in mind, and out the back door into the walled and wired garden behind the house.

"Why don't you let me use the wheelchair, Steve? This is silly."

"Because I'd rather carry you. Do you object? You know that you're as glad to get out of that motorized buggy for a while as I am to see you out. How do you feel today?" He deposited John with infinite care upon the cool grass.

"How should I feel? But tell me about your trouble."

"Quinn's campaign will be based on the fact that he claims I'm a robot."

John's eyes opened wide. "How do you know? It's impossible. I won't believe it."

"Oh, come, I tell you it's so. He had one of the big-shot scientists of U.S. Robot and Mechanical Men Corporation over at the office to argue with me."

Slowly John's hands tore at the grass. "I see. I see."

Byerly said, "But we can let him choose his ground. I have an idea. Listen to me and tell me if we can do it—"

The scene as it appeared in Alfred Lanning's office that night was a tableau of stares. Francis Quinn stared meditatively at Alfred Lanning. Lanning's stare was savagely set upon Susan Calvin, who stared impassively in her turn at Quinn.

Frances Quinn broke it with a heavy attempt at lightness. "Bluff. He's making it up as he goes along."

"Are you going to gamble on that, Mr. Quinn?" asked Dr. Calvin, indifferently.

"Well, it's your gamble, really."

"Look here." Lanning covered definite pessimism with bluster. "We've done what you asked. We witnessed the man eat. It's ridiculous to presume him a robot."

"Do *you* think so?" Quinn shot toward Calvin. "Lanning said you were the expert."

Lanning was almost threatening, "Now, Susan—"

Quinn interrupted smoothly, "Why not let her talk, man? She's been sitting there imitating a gatepost for half an hour."

Lanning felt definitely harassed. From what he experienced then to incipient paranoia was but a step. He said, "Very well. Have your say, Susan. We won't interrupt you."

Susan Calvin glanced at him humorlessly, then fixed cold eyes on Mr. Quinn. "There are only two ways of definitely proving Byerly to be a robot, sir. So far you are presenting circumstantial evidence, with which you can accuse, but not prove—and I think Mr. Byerly is sufficiently clever to counter that sort of material. You probably think so yourself, or you wouldn't have come here.

"The two methods of *proof* are the physical and the psychological. Physically, you can dissect him or use an X ray. How to do that would be *your* problem. Psychologically, his behavior can be studied, for if he *is* a positronic robot, he must conform to the three Rules of Robotics. A positronic brain cannot be constructed without them. You know the Rules, Mr. Quinn?"

She spoke them carefully, clearly, quoting word for word the famous bold print on page one of the *Handbook of Robotics*.

"I've heard of them," said Quinn, carelessly.

"Then the matter is easy to follow," responded the psychologist, dryly. "If Mr. Byerly breaks any of those three rules, he is not a robot. Unfortunately, this procedure works in only one direction. If he lives up to the rules, it proves nothing one way or the other."

Quinn raised polite eyebrows. "Why not, Doctor?"

"Because, if you stop to think of it, the three Rules of Robotics are the essential guiding principles of a good many of the world's ethical systems. Of course, every human being is supposed to have the instinct of self-preservation. That's Rule Three to a robot. Also every 'good' human being, with a social conscience and a sense of responsibility, is supposed to defer to proper authority; to listen to his doctor, his boss, his government, his psychiatrist, his fellow man; to obey laws, to follow rules, to conform to custom—even when they interfere with his comfort or safety. That's Rule Two to a robot. Also, every 'good' human being is supposed to love others as himself, protect his fellow man, risk his life to save another. That's Rule One to a robot. To put it simply—if Byerly follows all the Rules of Robotics, he may be a robot, and may simply be a very good man."

"But," said Quinn, "you're telling me that you can never prove him a robot."

"I may be able to prove him *not* a robot."

"That's not the proof I want."

"You'll have such proof as exists. You are the only one responsible for your own wants."

Here Lanning's mind leaped suddenly to the sting of an idea. "Has it occurred to anyone," he ground out, "that district attorney is a rather strange occupation for a robot? The prosecution of human beings—sentencing them to death—bringing about their infinite harm—"

Quinn grew suddenly keen. "No, you can't get out of it that way. Being district attorney doesn't make him human. Don't you know his record? Don't you know that he boasts that he has never prosecuted an innocent man; that there are scores of people left untried because the evidence against them didn't satisfy him, even though he could probably have argued a jury into atomizing them? That happens to be so."

Lanning's thin cheeks quivered. "No, Quinn, no. There is nothing in the Rules of Robotics that makes any allowance for human guilt. A robot may not judge whether a human being deserves death. It is not for him to decide. *He may not harm a human*—variety skunk, or variety angel."

Susan Calvin sounded tired. "Alfred," she said, "don't talk foolishly. What if a robot came upon a madman about to set fire to a house with people in it. He would stop the madman, wouldn't he?"

"Of course."

"And if the only way to stop him was to kill him—"

There was a faint sound in Lanning's throat. Nothing more.

"The answer to that, Alfred, is that he would do his best not to kill him. If the madman died, the robot would require psychotherapy because he might easily go mad at the conflict presented him—or having broken Rule One to adhere to Rule One in a higher sense. But a man would be dead and a robot would have killed him."

"Well, *is* Byerly mad?" demanded Lanning, with all the sarcasm he could muster.

"No, but he has killed no man himself. He has exposed facts which might represent a particular human being to be dangerous to a large mass of other human beings we call society. He protects the greater number and thus adheres to Rule One at maximum potential. That is as far as he goes. It is the judge who then condemns the criminal to death or imprisonment, after the jury decides on his guilt or innocence. It is the jailer who imprisons him, the executioner who kills him. And Mr. Byerly has done nothing but determine truth and aid society.

"As a matter of fact, Mr. Quinn, I have looked into Mr. Byerly's career since you first brought this matter to our attention. I find that he has never demanded the death sentence in his closing speeches to the jury. I also find that he has spoken on behalf of the abolition of capital punishment and contributed generously to research institutions engaged in criminal neurophysiology. He apparently believes in the cure, rather than the punishment of crime. I find that significant."

"You do?" Quinn smiled. "Significant of a certain odor of roboticity, perhaps?"

"Perhaps? Why deny it? Actions such as his could come only from a robot, or from a very honorable and decent human being. But you see, you just can't differentiate between a robot and the very best of humans."

Quinn sat back in his chair. His voice quivered with impatience. "Dr. Lanning, it's perfectly possible to create a humanoid robot that would perfectly duplicate a human in appearance, isn't it?"

Lanning harrumphed and considered. "It's been done experimentally by U.S. Robots," he said reluctantly, "without the addition of a positronic brain, of course. By using human ova and hormone control, one can grow human flesh and skin over a skeleton of porous silicone plastics that would defy external examination. The eyes, the hair, the skin would be really human, not humanoid. And if you put a positronic brain, and such other gadgets as you might desire inside, you have a humanoid robot.''

Quinn said shortly. "How long would it take to make one?"

Lanning considered, "If you had all your equipment—the brain, the skeleton, the ovum, the proper hormones and radiations—say, two months.''

The politician straightened out of his chair. "Then we shall see what the insides of Mr. Byerly look like. It will mean publicity for U.S. Robots—but I gave you your chance.''

Lanning turned impatiently to Susan Calvin, when they were alone. "Why do you insist—''

And with real feeling, she responded sharply and instantly, "Which do you want—the truth or my resignation? I won't lie for you. U.S. Robots can take care of itself. Don't turn coward.''

"What," said Lanning, "if he opens up Byerly, and wheels and gears fall out. What then?''

"He won't open Byerly," said Calvin, disdainfully. "Byerly is as clever as Quinn, at the very least.''

The news broke upon the city a week before Byerly was to have been nominated. But "broke" is the wrong word. It staggered upon the city, shambled, crawled. Laughter began, and wit was free. And as the far-off hand of Quinn tightened its pressure in easy stages, the laughter grew forced, an element of hollow uncertainty entered, and people broke off to wonder.

The convention itself had the air of a restive stallion. There had been no contest planned. Only Byerly could possibly have been nominated a week earlier. There was no substitute even now. They had to nominate him, but there was complete confusion about it.

It would not have been so bad if the average individual were not torn between the enormity of the charge, if true, and its sensational folly, if false.

The day after Byerly was nominated perfunctorily, hollowly—a newspaper finally published the gist of a long interview with Dr. Susan Calvin, "world-famous expert on robopsychology and positronics."

What broke loose is popularly and succinctly described as hell.

It was what the Fundamentalists were waiting for. They were not a political party; they made pretense to no formal religion. Essentially they were those who had not adapted themselves to what had been called the Atomic Age, in the days when atoms were a novelty. Actually, they were the Simple-Lifers, hungering after a life which to those who lived it had probably appeared not so Simple, and who had been, therefore, Simple-Lifers themselves.

The Fundamentalists required no new reason to detest robots and robot manufacturers; but a new reason such as the Quinn accusation and the Calvin analysis was sufficient to make such detestation audible.

The huge plant of the U.S. Robots and Mechanical Men Corporation was a hive that spawned armed guards. It prepared for war.

Within the city the house of Stephen Byerly bristled with police.

The political campaign, of course, lost all other issues, and resembled a campaign only in that it was something filling the hiatus between nomination and election.

Stephen Byerly did not allow the fussy little man to distract him. He remained comfortably unperturbed by the uniforms in the background. Outside the house, past the line of grim guards, reporters and photographers waited according to the tradition of the caste. One enterprising 'visor station even had a scanner focused on the blank entrance to the prosecutor's unpretentious home, while a synthetically excited announcer filled in with inflated commentary.

The fussy little man advanced. He held forward a rich, complicated sheet. "This, Mr. Byerly, is a court order authorizing me to search these premises for the presence of illegal . . . uh . . . mechanical men or robots of any description."

Byerly half rose and took the paper. He glanced at it indifferently, and smiled as he handed it back. "All in order. Go ahead. Do your job. Mrs. Hoppen"—to his housekeeper, who appeared reluctantly from the next room—"please go with them, and help out if you can."

The little man, whose name was Harroway, hesitated, produced an unmistakable blush, failed completely to catch Byerly's eyes, and muttered, "Come on," to the two policemen.

He was back in ten minutes.

"Through?" questioned Byerly, in just the tone of a person who is not particularly interested in the question or its answer.

Harroway cleared his throat, made a bad start in falsetto, and began again, angrily,"Look here, Mr. Byerly, our special instructions were to search the house very thoroughly."

"And haven't you?"

"We were told exactly what to look for."

"Yes?"

"In short, Mr. Byerly, and not to put too fine a point on it, we were told to search you."

"Me?" said the prosecutor with a broadening smile. "And how do you intend to do that?"

"We have a Penet-radiation unit—"

"Then I'm to have my X-ray photograph taken, hey? You have the authority?"

"You saw my warrant."

"May I see it again?"

Harroway, his forehead shining with considerably more than mere enthusiasm, passed it over a second time.

Byerly said evenly, "I read here as the description of what you are to search; I quote: 'the dwelling place belonging to Stephen Allen Byerly, located at 355 Willow Grove, Evanstron, together with any garage, storehouse or other structures or buildings thereto appertaining, together with all grounds thereto appertaining'... um... and so on. Quite in order. But, my good man, it doesn't say anything about searching my interior. I am not part of the premises. You may search my clothes if you think I've got a robot hidden in my pocket."

Harroway had no doubt on the point of to whom he owed his job. He did not propose to be backward, given a chance to earn a much better—i.e., more highly paid—job.

He said, in a faint echo of bluster, "Look here. I'm allowed to search the furniture in your house, and anything else I find in it. You are in it, aren't you?"

"A remarkable observation. I *am* in it. But I'm not a piece of furniture. As a citizen of adult reponsibility—I have the psychiatric certificate proving that—I have certain rights under the Regional Articles. Searching me would come under the heading of violating my Right of Privacy. That paper isn't sufficient."

"Sure, but if you're a robot, you don't have a Right of Privacy."

"True enough—but that paper still isn't sufficient. It recognizes me implicitly as a human being."

"Where?" Harroway snatched at it.

"Where it says, 'the dwelling place belonging to' and so on. A robot cannot own property. And you may tell your employer, Mr. Harroway, that if he tries to issue a similar paper which does *not* implicitly recognize me as a human being, he will be immediately faced with a restraining injunction and a civil suit which will make it necessary for him to *prove* me a robot by means of information *now* in his possession, or else to pay a whopping penalty for an attempt to deprive me unduly of my rights under the Regional Articles. You'll tell him that, won't you?''

Harroway marched to the door. He turned. ''You're a slick lawyer—'' His hand was in his pocket. For a short moment, he stood there. Then he left, smiled in the direction of the 'visor scanner, still playing away—waved to the reporters, and shouted, ''We'll have something for you tomorrow, boys. No kidding.''

In his ground car, he settled back, removed the tiny mechanism from his pocket and carefully inspected it. It was the first time he had ever taken a photograph by X-ray reflection. He hoped he had done it correctly.

Quinn and Byerly had never met face-to-face alone. But visorphone was pretty close to it. In fact, accepted literally, perhaps the phrase was accurate, even if to each, the other was merely the light-and-dark pattern of a bank of photocells.

It was Quinn who had initiated the call. It was Quinn who spoke first, and without particular ceremony. ''Thought you would like to know, Byerly, that I intend to make public the fact that you're wearing a protective shield against Penet-radiation.''

''That so? In that case, you've probably already made it public. I have a notion our enterprising press representatives have been tapping my various communications lines for quite a while. I know they have my office lines full of holes; which is why I've dug in at my home these last weeks.'' Byerly was friendly, almost chatty.

Quinn's lips tightened lightly, ''This call is shielded—thoroughly. I'm making it at a certain personal risk.''

"So I should imagine. Nobody knows you're behind this campaign. At least, nobody knows it officially. Nobody doesn't know it unofficially. I wouldn't worry. So I wear a protective shield. I suppose you found that out when your puppy dog's Penet-radiation photograph, the other day, turned out to be overexposed."

"You realize, Byerly, that it would be pretty obvious to everyone that you don't dare face X-ray analysis."

"Also that you, or your men, attempted illegal invasion of my Right of Privacy."

"The devil they'll care for that."

"They might. It's rather symbolic of our two campaigns, isn't it? You have little concern with the rights of the individual citizen. I have great concern. I will not submit to X-ray analysis, because I wish to maintain my rights on principle. Just as I'll maintain the rights of others when elected."

"That will no doubt make a very interesting speech, but no one will believe you. A little too high-sounding to be true. Another thing." A sudden, crisp change. "The personnel in your home was not complete the other night."

"In what way?"

"According to the report," he shuffled papers before him that were just within the range of the visiplate, "there was one person missing—a cripple."

"As you say," said Byerly, tonelessly, "a cripple. My old teacher, who lives with me and who is now in the country—and has been for two months. A 'much-needed rest' is the usual expression applied in the case. He has your permission?"

"Your teacher? A scientist of sorts?"

"A lawyer once—before he was a cripple. He has a government license as a research biophysicist, with a laboratory of his own, and a complete description of the work he's doing filed with the proper authorities, to whom I refer you. The work is minor, but is a harmless and engaging hobby for a—poor cripple. I am being as helpful as I can, you see.''

''I see. And what does this . . . teacher . . . know about robot manufacture?''

''I couldn't judge the extent of his knowledge in a field with which I am unacquainted.''

''He wouldn't have access to positronic brains?''

''Ask your friends at U.S. Robots. They'd be the ones to know.''

''I'll put it shortly, Byerly. Your crippled teacher is the real Stephen Byerly. You are his robot creation. We can prove it. It was he who was in the automobile accident, not you. There will be ways of checking the records.''

''Really? Do so, then. My best wishes.''

''And we can search your so-called teacher's 'country place,' and see what we can find there.''

''Well, not quite, Quinn.'' Byerly smiled broadly. ''Unfortunately for you, my so-called teacher is a sick man. His country place is his place of rest. His Right of Privacy as a citizen of adult responsibility is naturally even stronger, under the circumstances. You won't be able to obtain a warrant to enter his grounds without showing just cause. However, I'd be the last to prevent you from trying.''

There was a pause of moderate length, and then Quinn leaned forward, so that his imaged-face expanded and the fine lines on his forehead were visible, ''Byerly, why do you carry on? You can't be elected.''

''Can't I?''

''Do you think you can? Do you suppose that your failure to make any attempt to disprove the robot charge—when you could easily, by breaking one of the Three Laws—does anything but convince the people that you *are* a robot?''

''All I see so far is that from being a rather vaguely known, but still largely obscure metropolitan lawyer, I have now become a world figure. You're a good publicist.''

''But you *are* a robot.''

''So it's been said, but not proven.''

''It's been proven sufficiently for the electorate.''

''Then relax—you've won.''

''Good-bye,'' said Quinn, with his first touch of viciousness, and the visorphone slammed off.

''Good-bye,'' said Byerly imperturbably, to the blank plate.

Byerly brought his ''teacher'' back the week before election. The air car dropped quickly in an obscure part of the city.

''You'll stay here till after election,'' Byerly told him. ''It would be better to have you out of the way if things take a bad turn.''

The hoarse voice that twisted painfully out of John's crooked mouth might have had accents of concern in it. ''There's danger of violence?''

''The Fundamentalists threaten it, so I suppose there is, in a theoretical sense. But I really don't expect it. The Fundies have no real power. They're just the continuous irritant factor that might stir up a riot after a while. You don't mind staying here? Please. I won't be myself if I have to worry about you.''

''Oh, I'll stay. You still think it will go well?''

''I'm sure of it. No one bothered you at the place?''

''No one. I'm certain.''

''And your part went well?''

''Well enough. There'll be no trouble there.''

''Then take care of yourself, and watch the televisor tomorrow, John.'' Byerly pressed the gnarled hand that rested on his own.

Lenton's forehead was a furrowed study in suspense. He had the completely unenviable job of being Byerly's campaign manager in a campaign that wasn't a campaign, for a person that refused to reveal his strategy, and refused to accept his manager's.

"You can't!" It was his favorite phrase. It had become his only phrase. "I tell you, Steve, you can't!"

He threw himself in front of the prosecutor, who was spending his time leafing through the typed pages of his speech.

"Put that down, Steve. Look, that mob has been organized by Fundies. You won't get a hearing. You'll be stoned more likely. Why do you have to make a speech before an audience? What's wrong with a recording, a visual recording?"

"You want me to win the election, don't you?" asked Byerly, mildly.

"Win the election! You're not going to win, Steve. I'm trying to save your life."

"Oh, I'm not in danger."

"He's not in danger. He's not in danger." Lenton made a queer, rasping sound in his throat. "You mean you're getting out on that balcony in front of fifty thousand crackpots and try to talk sense to them—on a balcony like a medieval dictator?"

Byerly consulted his watch. "In about five minutes—as soon as the television lines are free."

Lenton's answering remark was not quite transliterable.

The crowds filled a roped-off area of the city. Trees and houses seemed to grow out of a mass-human foundation. And by ultrawave, the rest of the world watched. It was a purely local election, but it had a world audience just the same. Byerly thought of that and smiled.

But there was nothing to smile at in the crowd itself. There were banners and streamers, ringing every possible change on his supposed robotcy. The hostile attitude rose thickly and tangibly into the atmosphere.

From the start the speech was not successful. It competed

against the inchoate mob howl and the rhythmic cries of the Fundie claques that formed mob-islands within the mob. Byerly spoke on, slowly, unemotionally—

Inside, Lenton clutched his hair and groaned—and waited for the blood.

There was a writhing in the front ranks. An angular citizen with popping eyes, and clothes too short for the lank length of his limbs, was pulling to the fore. A policeman dived after him, making slow, struggling passage. Byerly waved the latter off, angrily.

The thin man was directly under the balcony. His words tore unheard against the roar.

Byerly leaned forward. "What do you say? If you have a legitimate question, I'll answer it." He turned to a flanking guard. "Bring that man up here."

There was a tensing in the crowd. Cries of "Quiet" started in various parts of the mob, and rose to a bedlam, then toned down raggedly. The thin man, red-faced and panting, faced Byerly.

Byerly said, "Have you a question?"

The thin man stared, and said in a cracked voice, "Hit me!"

With sudden energy, he thrust out his chin at an angle. "Hit me! You say you're not a robot. Prove it. You can't hit me, you monster."

There was a queer, flat, dead silence. Byerly's voice punctured it. "I have no reason to hit you."

The thin man was laughing wildly. "You *can't* hit me. You *won't* hit me. You're not a human. You're a monster, a make-believe man."

And Stephen Byerly, tight-lipped, in the face of thousands who watched in person and the millions who watched by screen, drew back his fist and caught the man crackingly under the chin.

The challenger went over backwards in sudden collapse, with nothing on his face but blank, blank surprise.

Byerly said, "I'm sorry. Take him in and see that he's comfortable. I want to speak with him when I'm through."

And when Dr. Calvin, from her reserved space, turned her automobile and drove off, only one reporter had recovered sufficiently from the shock to race after her, and shout an unheard question.

Susan Calvin called over her shoulder, "He's human."

That was enough. The reporter raced away in his own direction.

The rest of the speech might be described as "Spoken but not heard."

Dr. Calvin and Stephen Byerly met once again—a week before he took the oath of office as mayor. It was late—past midnight.

Dr. Calvin said, "You don't look tired."

The mayor-elect smiled. "I may stay up for a while. Don't tell Quinn."

"I shan't. But that was an interesting story of Quinn's. It's a shame to have spoiled it. I suppose you knew his theory?"

"Parts of it."

"It was highly dramatic. Stephen Byerly was a young lawyer, a powerful speaker, a great idealist—and with a certain flair for biophysics. Are you interested in robotics, Mr. Byerly?"

"Only in the legal aspects."

"*This* Stephen Byerly was. But there was an accident. Byerly's wife died; he himself, worse. His legs were gone; his face was gone; his voice was gone. Part of his mind was—bent. He would not submit to plastic surgery. He retired from the world, legal career gone—only his intelligence and his hands left.

Somehow he could obtain positronic brains, even a complex one, one which had the greatest capacity of forming judgments in ethical problems—which is the highest robotic function so far developed.

"He grew a body about it. Trained it to be everything he would have been and was no longer. He sent it out into the world as Stephen Byerly, remaining behind himself as the old, crippled teacher that no one ever saw—"

"Unfortunately," said the mayor-elect, "I ruined all that by hitting a man. The papers say it was your official verdict on the occasion that I was human."

"How did that happen? Do you mind telling me? It couldn't have been accidental."

"It wasn't entirely. Quinn did most of the work. My men started quietly spreading the fact that I had never hit a man; that I was unable to hit a man; that to fail to do so under provocation would be sure proof that I was a robot. So I arranged for a silly speech in public, with all sorts of publicity overtones, and almost inevitably, some fool fell for it. In its essence, it was what I call a shyster trick. One in which the artificial atmosphere which has been created does all the work. Of course, the emotional effects made my election certain, as intended."

The robopsychologist nodded. "I see you intrude upon my field—as every politician must, I suppose. But I'm very sorry it turned out this way. I like robots. I like them considerably better than I do human beings. If a robot can be created capable of being a civil executive, I think he'd make the best one possible. By the Laws of Robotics, he'd be incapable of corruption, of stupidity, of prejudice. And after he had served a decent term, he would leave, even though he was immortal, because it would be impossible for him to hurt humans by letting them know that a robot had ruled them. It would be most ideal."

"Except that a robot might fail due to the inherent inadequacies of his brain. The positronic brain has never equaled the complexities of the human brain.''

''He would have advisers. Not even a human brain is capable of governing without assistance.''

Byerly considered Susan Calvin with grave interest. ''Why do you smile, Dr. Calvin?''

''I smile because Mr. Quinn didn't think of everything.''

''You mean there could be more to that story of his.''

''Only a little. For the three months before election, this Stephen Byerly that Mr. Quinn spoke about, this broken man, was in the country for some mysterious reason. He returned in time for that famous speech of yours. And after all, what the cripple did once, he could do a second time, particularly where the second job is very simple in comparison to the first.''

''I don't quite understand.''

Dr. Calvin rose and smoothed her dress. She was obviously ready to leave. ''I mean there is one time when a robot may strike a human being without breaking the First Law. Just one time.''

''And when is that?''

Dr. Calvin was at the door. She said quietly, ''When the human to be struck is merely another robot.''

She smiled broadly, her thin face glowing. ''Good-bye, Mr. Byerly. I hope to vote for you five years from now—for co-ordinator.''

Stephen Byerly chuckled. ''I must reply that that is a somewhat farfetched idea.''

The door closed behind her.

MADE IN U.S.A.

J. T. McIntosh

"J. T. McIntosh" is the pseudonym under which James Murdoch MacGregor has written science fiction for the past quarter of a century. Mr. MacGregor, you will not be surprised to learn, is a Scot, born in Paisley and for many years a resident of Aberdeen. He has been a journalist, a professional musician, and a free-lance writer, and his science fiction, with a strong emphasis on the complexities of human relationships, won him a wide following in the 1950's with such outstanding novels as One in Three Hundred, World Out of Mind, *and* Born Leader. *There have been few McIntosh stories in recent years, but word has it that he is writing once again—good news indeed.*

I

Not a soul watched as Roderick Liffcom carried his bride across the threshold. They were just a couple of nice, good-looking kids—Roderick a psychologist and Alison an ex-copy-writer. They weren't news yet. There was nothing to hint that in a few days the name of Liffcom would be known to almost everyone in the world, the tag on a case which interested everybody. Not everyone would follow a murder case, a graft case, or an espionage case. But everyone would follow the Liffcom case.

Let's have a good look at them while we have the chance, before the mobs surround them. Roderick was big and strong enough to treat his wife's 115 pounds with contempt, but there was no contempt in the way he held her. He carried her as if she were a million dollars in small bills and there were a strong wind blowing. He looked down at her with his heart in his eyes. He had black hair and brown eyes and one could see at a glance that he could have carried any girl he liked over the threshold.

Alison nestled in his arms like a kitten, eyes half-closed with rapture, arms about his neck. She was blond and had fantastically beautiful eyes, not to mention the considerable claims to notice of her other features. But even at first glance one would know that there was more to Alison than beauty. It might be brains, or courage, or hard, bitter experience that had tempered her keen as steel. One could see at a glance that she could have been carried over the threshold by any man she liked.

As they went in, it was the end of a story. But let's be different and call it the beginning.

In the morning, when they were at breakfast on the terrace, the picture hadn't changed radically. That is, Roderick was rather different, blue-chinned and sleepy-eyed and in a brown flannel bathrobe, and Alison was more spectacularly different in a pale-green negligee that wasn't so much worn as wafted about. But the way they looked at each other hadn't changed remotely—then.

"There's something," remarked Alison casually, tracing patterns on the damask tablecloth with one slim finger, "that perhaps I ought to tell you."

Two minutes later they were fighting for the phone.

"I want to call my lawyer," Roderick bellowed.

"I want to call my lawyer," Alison retorted.

He paused, the number half dialed. "You can't," he told her roughly. "It's the same lawyer."

She recovered herself first, as she always had. She smiled sunnily. "Shall we toss a coin for him?" she suggested.

"No," said Roderick brutally. Where, oh, where was his great blinding love? "He's mine. I pay him more than you ever could."

"Right," agreed Alison. "I'll fight the case myself."

"So will I," Roderick exclaimed, and slammed the receiver down. Instantly he picked it up again. "No, we'll need him to get things moving."

"Collusion?" asked Alison sweetly.

"It was a low, mean, stinking, dirty, cattish, obscene, disgusting, filthy-minded thing to wait until . . ."

"Until what?" Alison asked with more innocence than one would have thought there was in the world.

"Android!" he spat viciously at her.

Despite herself, her eyes flashed with anger.

II

The newspapers not only mentioned it, they said it at the top of their voices: HUMAN SUES ANDROID FOR DIVORCE. It wasn't much of a headline, for one naturally wondered why a human suing an android for divorce should rate a front-page story. Every day humans divorced humans, humans androids, androids humans, and androids androids. The natural reaction to a headline like that was : "So what? Who cares?"

But it didn't need particular intelligence to realize that there must be something rather special about this case.

The report ran:

Everton, Tuesday. History is made today in the first human vs. android divorce case since the recent grant of

full legal equality to androids. It is also the first case
of a divorce sought on the grounds that one contracting
party did not know the other was an android. This became possible only because the equality law made it no
longer obligatory to disclose android origin in any con-
tract.

Recognizing the importance of this test case, certain to
affect millions in the future, *Twenty-four Hours* will cover
the case, which opens on Friday, in meticulous detail. Ace
reporters Anona Grier and Walter Hallsmith will bring to
our readers the whole story of this historic trial. Grier is
human and Hallsmith android . . .

The report went on to give such details as the names of the
people in this important test case, and remarked incidentally that
although the Liffcom marriage had lasted only ten hours and
thirteen minutes before the divorce plea was entered, there had
been even briefer marriages recorded.

Twenty-four Hours thus adroitly obviated thousands of letters
asking breathlessly: "Is this a record?"

III

Alison, back at her bachelor flat, stretched herself on a divan,
focused her eyes past the ceiling on infinity, and thought and
thought and thought.

She wasn't particularly unhappy. Not for Alison were misery
and resentment and wild, impossible hope. She met the tragedy
of her life with placid resignation and even humor.

"Let's face it," she told herself firmly. "I'm hurt. I hoped
he'd say. 'It doesn't matter. What difference could that make?
It's you I love'—the sort of thing men say in love stories. But
what did he say? *Dirty Android.*"

Oh, well. Life wasn't like love stories or they wouldn't just be
stories.

She might as well admit for a start that she still loved him. That would clarify her feelings.

She should have told him earlier that she was an android. Perhaps he had some excuse for believing she merely waited until non-consummation was no longer ground for divorce, and then triumphantly threw the fact that she was an android in his lap. (But what good was that supposed to do her?)

It wasn't like that at all, of course. She hadn't told him because they had to get to know each other before the question arose. One didn't say the moment one was introduced to a person: "I'm married," or "I once served five years for theft," or "I'm an android. Are you?"

If in the first few weeks she had known Roderick, some remark had been made about androids, she'd have remarked that she was one herself. But it never had.

When he asked her to marry him she honestly didn't think of saying she was an android. There were times when it mattered and times when it didn't; this seemed to be one of the latter. Roderick was so intelligent, so liberal minded, and so easygoing (except when he lost his temper) that she didn't think he would care.

It never did occur to her that he might care. She just mentioned it, as one might say: "I hope you don't mind my drinking iced coffee every morning." Well, almost. She just mentioned it . . .

And happiness was over.

Now an idea was growing in the sad ripple of her thoughts. Did Roderick really want this divorce case, after all, or was he only trying to prove something? Because if he was, she was ready to admit cheerfully that it was proved.

She wanted Roderick. She didn't quite understand what had happened—perhaps he would take her back on condition that he could trample on her face first. If so, that was all right. She was prepared to let him swear at her and rage at androids and work off any prejudice and hate he might have accumulated somehow, somewhere—as long as he took her back.

She reached behind her, picked up the telephone and dialed Roderick's number.

"Hello, Roderick," she said cheerfully. "This is Alison. No, don't hang up. Tell me, why do you hate androids?"

There was such a long silence that she knew he was considering everything, including the advisability of hanging up without a word. It could be said of Roderick that he thought things through very carefully before going off half-cocked.

"I don't hate androids," he barked at last.

"You've got something against android girls, then?"

"No!" he shouted. "I'm a psychologist. I think comparatively straight. I'm not fouled up with race hatred and prejudice and megalomania and—"

"Then," said Alison very quietly, "it's just one particular android girl you hate."

Roderick's voice was suddenly quiet, too. "No, Alison. It has nothing to do with that. It's just . . . children."

So that was it. Alison's eyes filled with tears. That was the one thing she could do nothing about, the thing she had refused even to consider.

"You really mean it?" she asked. "That's not just the case you're going to make out?"

"It's the case I'm going to make out," he replied, "and I mean it. Trouble is, Alison, you hit something you couldn't have figured on. Most people want children, but are resigned to the fact that they're not likely to get them. I was one of a family of eight. The youngest. You'd have thought, wouldn't you, that the line was pretty safe?

"Well, all the others are married. Some have been for a long time. One brother and two sisters have been married twice. That makes a total of seventeen human beings, not counting me. And their net achievement in the way of reproduction is zero.

"It's a question of family continuity, don't you see? I don't think we'd mind if there was *one* child among the lot of us—*one* extension into the future. But there isn't, and there's only this chance left."

Alison dropped as close to misery as she ever did. She understood every word Roderick said and what was behind every word. If she ever had a chance of having children, she wouldn't give it up for one individual or love of one individual, either.

But then, of course, she never had it.

In the silence, Roderick hung up. Alison looked down at her own beautiful body and for once couldn't draw a shadow of complacency or content from looking at it. Instead, it irritated her, for it would never produce a child. What was the use of all the appearance, all the mechanism of sex, without its one real function?

But it never occurred to her to give up, to let the suit go undefended. There must be something she could do, some line she could take. Winning the case was nothing, except that that might be a tiny, unimportant part of winning back Roderick.

IV

The judge was a little pompous, and it was obvious from the start that under the very considerable power he had under the contract-court system, he meant to run this case in his own way and enjoy it.

He clasped his hands on the bench and looked around the packed courtroom happily. He made his introductory remarks with obvious intense satisfaction that at least fifty reporters were writing down every word.

"This has been called an important case," he said, "and it is.

I could tell you why it is important, but that would not be justice. Our starting point must be this.'' He wagged his head in solemn glee at the jury. ''We know nothing.''

He liked that. He said it again. *''We know nothing.* We don't know the factors involved. We have never heard of androids. All this and more, we have to be told. We can call on anyone anywhere for evidence. And we must make up our minds *here* and *now,* on what we are told *here* and *now,* on the rights and wrongs of this case—and on nothing else.''

He had stated his theme and he developed it. He swooped and soared; he shot out of sight and returned like a swift raven to cast pearls before swine. For, of course, his audience was composed of swine. He didn't say so or drop the smallest hint to that effect, but it wasn't necessary. Only on Roderick and Alison did he cast a fatherly, friendly eye. They had given him his hour of glory. They weren't swine.

But Judge Collier was no fool. Before he had lost the interest he had created, he was back in the courtroom, getting things moving.

''I understand,'' he said, glancing from Alison to Roderick and then back to Alison, which was understandable, ''that you are conducting your own cases. That will be a factor tending toward informality, which is all to the good. First of all, will you look at the jury?''

Everyone in court looked at the jury. The jury looked at each other. In accordance with contract-court procedure, Roderick and Alison faced each other across the room, with the jury behind Alison so that they could see Roderick full-face and Alison in profile, and would know when they were lying.

''Alison Liffcom,'' said the judge, ''have you any objection to any member of the jury?''

Alison studied them. They were people, no more, no less.

Careful police surveys produced juries that were as near to genuine random groups as could reasonably be found.

"No," she said.

"Roderick Liffcom. Have you any objection—"

"Yes," said Roderick belligerently. "I want to know how many of them are androids."

There was a stir of interest in the court.

So it was really to be a human-android battle.

Judge Collier's expression did not change. "Out of order," he said. "Humans and androids are equal at law, and you cannot object to any juror because he is an android."

"But this case concerns the rights of humans and androids," Roderick protested.

"It concerns nothing of the kind," replied the judge sternly, "and if your plea is along those lines, we may as well forget the whole thing and go home. You cannot divorce your wife because she is an android."

"But she didn't tell me—"

"Nor because she didn't tell you. No android now is obliged, ever, to disclose—"

"I know all that," said Roderick, exasperated. "Must I state the obvious? I never had much to do with the law, but I do know this—the fact that *A* equals *B* may cut no ice, while the fact that *B* equals *A* may sew the whole case up. Okay, I'll state the obvious. I seek divorce on the grounds that Alison concealed from me until after our marriage her inability to have a child."

It was the obvious plea, but it was still a surprise to some people. There was a murmur of interest. Now things could move. There was something to argue about.

Alison watched Roderick and smiled at the thought that she knew him much better than anyone else in the courtroom did. Calm, he was dangerous, and he was fighting to be calm. And as she looked steadily at him, part of her was wondering how she could upset him and put him off stroke, while the other part was praying that he would be able to control himself and show up well.

She was asked to take the stand and she did it absentmindedly, still thinking about Roderick. Yes, she contested the divorce. No, she didn't deny the facts as stated. On what grounds did she contest the case, then?

She brought her attention back to the matter in hand. "Oh, that's very simple. I can put it in—" she counted on her fingers—"nine words. How do we know I can't have a child?"

Reporters wrote down the word "sensation." It wouldn't have lasted, but Alison knew that. She piled on more fuel.

"I'm not stating my whole case," she said. "All I'm saying at the moment is . . ." She blushed. She felt it on her face and was pleased with herself. She hadn't been sure she could do it. "I don't like to speak of such things, but I suppose I must. When I married Roderick, I was a virgin. How could I possibly know then that I couldn't have a baby?"

V

It took a long time to get things back to normal after that. The judge had to exhaust himself hammering with his gavel and threatening to clear the court. But Alison caught Roderick's eye, and he grinned and shook his head slowly. Roderick was two people, at least. He was the hothead, quick to anger, impulsive, emotional. But he was also, though it was hard to believe sometimes, a psychologist, able to sift and weigh and classify things and decide what they meant.

She knew what he meant as he shook his head at her. She had made a purely artificial point, effective only for the moment. She knew she was an android and that androids didn't have children. The rest was irrelevant.

"We have now established," the judge was saying, breathless from shouting and banging with his gavel, "what the case is about and some of the facts. Alison Liffcom admits that she concealed the fact that she was an android, as she was perfectly entitled to do—" He frowned down at Roderick, who had risen. "Well?"

Roderick, at the moment, was the psychologist. "You mentioned the word 'android,' Judge. Have you forgotten that none of us knows what an android is? You said, I believe, 'We have never heard of androids.' "

Judge Collier clearly preferred the other Roderick, whom he could squash when he liked. "Precisely," he said without enthusiasm. "Do you propose to tell us?"

"I propose to have you told," said Roderick.

Dr. Geller took the stand. Roderick faced him, looking calm and competent. Most of the audience were women. He knew how to make the most of himself, and he did. Dr. Geller, silver-haired, dignified, was as impassive as a statue.

"Who are you, Doctor?" asked Roderick coolly.

"I am director of the Everton Creche, where the androids for the entire state are made."

"You know quite a bit about androids?"

"I do."

"Just incidentally, in case anyone would like to know, do you mind telling us whether you are human or android?"

"Not at all. I am an android."

"I see. Now perhaps you'll tell us what androids are, when they were first made, and why?"

"Androids are just people. No different from humans except that they're made instead of born. I take it you don't want me to tell you the full details of the process. Basically, one starts with a few living cells—that's always necessary—and gradually forms a complete human body. There is no difference. I must stress that. An android is a man or a woman, not in any sense a robot or automaton.''

There was a stir again, and the judge smiled faintly. Roderick's witness looked like something of a burden to Roderick. But Roderick merely nodded. Everything, apparently, was under control.

"About two hundred years ago,'' the doctor went on, "it was shown beyond reasonable doubt that the human race was headed for extinction fairly soon. The population was halving itself every generation. Even if human life continued, civilization could not be maintained . . .''

It was dull for everybody. Even Dr. Geller didn't seem very interested in what he was saying. This was the part everyone knew already. But the judge didn't interfere. It was all strictly relevant.

At first the androids had only been an experiment, interesting because they were from the first an astonishingly successful experiment. There was little failure, and a lot of startling success. Once the secret was discovered, one could, by artificial means, manufacture creatures who were men and women to the last decimal point. There was only one tiny flaw. They couldn't reproduce, either among themselves or with human partners. Everything was normal except that conception never took place.

But as the human population dropped, and as the public services slowed, became inefficient, or closed down, it was natural that the bright idea should occur to someone: Why shouldn't the androids do it?

So androids were made and trained as public servants. At first they were lower than the beasts. But that, to do humanity justice, lasted only until it became clear that androids were people. Then androids ascended the social scale to the exalted level of slaves. The curious thing, however, was that there was only one way to make androids, and that was to make them as babies and let them grow up. It wasn't possible to make only stupid, imperfect, adult androids. They turned out like humans, good, bad and indifferent.

And then came the transformation.' Human births took an upsurge. It was renaissance. There was even unemployment for a while again. It would have been inhuman, of course, to kill off the androids, but on the other hand, if anyone was going to starve, they might as well.

They did.

No more androids were made. Human births subsided. Androids were manufactured again. Human births rose.

It became obvious at last. The human race had not so much been extinguishing itself with birth control as actually failing to reproduce. Most people, men and women, were barren these days. But a certain percentage of this barrenness was psychological. The androids were a challenge. They stimulated a stubborn strain deep in humans.

So a balance was reached. Androids were made for two reasons only—to have that challenging effect that kept the human race holding its ground, almost replacing its losses, and to do all the dirty work of keeping a juggernaut of an economic system functioning smoothly for a decimated population.

Even in the early days, the androids had champions. Curiously enough, it wasn't a matter of the androids fighting for and winning equality, but of humans fighting among each other and gradually giving the androids equality.

The humans who fought most were those who couldn't have children. All these people could do if they were to have a family was adopt baby androids. Naturally they lavished on them all the affection and care their own children would have had. They came to look on them as their own children. They therefore were very strongly in favor of any move to remove restrictions on androids. One's own son or daughter shouldn't be treated as an inferior being.

That was some of the story, as Dr. Geller sketched it. The court was restive, the judge looked at the ceiling, the jury looked at Alison. Only Roderick was politely attentive to Dr. Geller.

VI

Everyone knew at once when the lull was over. If anyone missed Roderick's question, no one missed the doctor's answer: "—reasonably established that androids cannot reproduce. At first there was actually some fear that they might. It was thought that the offspring of android and human would be some kind of monster. But reproduction did not occur."

"Just one more point, Doctor," said Roderick easily. "There is, I understand, some method of identification—some means of telling human from android, and vice versa?"

"There are two," replied the doctor. Some of the people in court looked up, interested. Others made their indifference obvious to show that they knew what was coming. "The first is the fingerprint system. It is just as applicable to androids as to humans, and every android at every creche is fingerprinted. If for any reason it becomes necessary to identify a person who may or may not be android, prints are taken. Once these have been sent to every main android center in the world—a process which only takes two weeks—the person is either positively identified as android or by elimination is known to be human."

"There is no possibility of error?"

"There is always the possibility of error. The system is perfect, but to err is human—and, if I may be permitted the pleasantry, android as well."

"Quite," said Roderick. "But may we take it that the possibility of error in this case is small?"

"You may. As for the other method of identification: this is a relic of the early days of android manufacture and many of us feel—but that is not germane.''

For the first time, however, he looked somewhat uncomfortable as he went on: ''Androids, of course, are not born. There is no umbilical cord. The navel is small, even and symmetrical, and faintly but quite clearly marked inside it are the words—in this country, at any rate—'Made in U.S.A.' ''

A wave of sniggers ran round the court. The doctor flushed faintly. There were jokes about the little stamp that all androids carried. Once there had been political cartoons with the label as the motif. The point of one allegedly funny story came when it was discovered that a legend which was expected to be 'Made in U.S.A.' turned out to be 'Fabriqué en France' instead.

It had always been something humans could jibe about, the stamp that every android would carry on his body to his grave. Twenty years ago, all persecution of androids was over, supposedly, and androids were free and accepted and had all but the same rights as humans. Yet twenty years ago, women's evening dress invariably revealed the navel, whatever else was chastely concealed. Human girls flaunted the fact that they were human. Android girls either meekly showed the proof, or, by hiding it, admitted they were android.

''There is under review,'' said the doctor, ''a proposal to discontinue what some people feel must always be a badge of subservience—''

''That is *sub judice*,'' interrupted the judge, ''and no part of the matter in question. We are concerned with things as they are.'' He looked inquiringly at Roderick. ''Have you finished with the witness?''

''Not only the witness,'' said Roderick, ''but my case.'' He looked so pleased with himself that Alison, who was difficult to anger, wanted to hit him. ''You have heard Dr. Geller's evidence. I demand that Alison submit herself to the two tests he mentioned. When it is established that she is an android, it will also be established that she cannot have a child. And that she therefore, by concealing her android status from me, also concealed the fact that she could not have a child.''

The judge nodded somewhat reluctantly. He looked over his glasses at Alison without much hope. It would be a pity if such a promising case were allowed to fizzle out so soon and so trivially. But he personally could see nothing significant that Alison could offer in rebuttal.

''Your witness,'' said Roderick, with a gesture that called for a kick in the teeth, or so Alison thought.

''Thank you,'' she said sweetly. She rose from her seat and crossed the floor. She wore a plain gray suit with a vivid yellow blouse, only a little of it visible, supplying the necessary touch of color. She had never looked better in her life and she knew it.

Roderick looked as though he were losing the iron control which he had held for so long against all her expectations, and she did what she could to help by wriggling her skirt straight in the way he had always found so attractive.

''Stop that!'' he hissed at her. ''This is serious.''

She merely showed him twenty-eight of her perfect teeth, and then turned to Dr. Geller.

VII

''I was most interested in a phrase you used, Doctor,'' said Alison. ''You said it was 'reasonably established' that androids could not reproduce. Now I take it I have the facts correct. You are director of the Everton Creche?''

''Yes.''

''And your professional experience is therefore confined to androids up to the age of ten?

"Is it usual for even humans," asked Allison, "to reproduce before the age of ten?"

There was a stunned silence, then a laugh, then applause. "This is not a radio show," shouted the judge. "Proceed, if you please, Mrs. Liffcom."

Alison did. Dr. Geller was the right man to come to for all matters relating to *young* androids, she said apologetically, but for matters relating to adult androids (no offense to Dr. Geller intended, of course), she proposed to call Dr. Smith.

Roderick interrupted. He was perfectly prepared to hear Alison's case, but hadn't they better conclude his first? Was Alison prepared to submit herself to the two tests mentioned?

"It's unnecessary," said Alison. "I am an android. I am not denying it."

"Nevertheless—" said Roderick.

"I don't quite understand, Mr. Liffcom," the judge put in. "If there were any doubt, yes. But Mrs. Liffcom is not claiming that she is not an android."

"I want to *know*."

"Do you think there is any doubt?"

"I only wish there were."

It was "sensation" again.

"And yet it's all perfectly natural, when you consider it," said Roderick, when he could be heard. "I want a divorce because Alison is an android and can't have a child. If she's been mistaken, or has been playing some game, or whatever it might be, I don't want a divorce. I want Alison, the girl I married. Surely that's easy enough to understand?"

"All right," said Alison emotionlessly. "It'll take some time to check my fingerprints, but the other test can be made now. What do I do, Judge, peel here in front of everybody?"

"Great Scott, no!"

Five minutes later, in the jury room, the judge, the jury, and

Roderick examined the proof. Alison surrendered none of her dignity of self-possession while showing it to them.

There was no doubt. The mark of the android was perfectly clear.

Roderick was last to look. When he had examined the brand, his eyes met Alison's, and she had to fight back the tears. For he wasn't satisfied or angry, only sorry.

Back in court, Roderick said he waived the fingerprint test. And Alison called Dr. Smith. He was older than Dr. Geller, but bright-eyed and alert. There was something about him—people leaned forward as he took the stand, knowing somehow that what he had to say was going to be worth hearing.

"Following the procedure of my learned friend," said Alison, "may I ask you if you are human or android, Dr. Smith?"

"You may. I am human. However, most of my patients have been android."

"Why is that?"

"Because I realized long ago that androids represented the future. Humans are losing the fight. That being so, I wanted to find out what the differences between humans and androids were, or if there were any at all. If there were none, so much the better—the human race wasn't going to die out, after all."

"But of course," said Alison casually, yet somehow everyone hung on her words, "there was one essential difference. Humanity was becoming sterile, but androids couldn't reproduce."

"There was no difference," said Dr. Smith.

Sometimes an unexpected statement produces silence, sometimes bedlam. Dr. Smith got both in turn. There was the stillness of shock as he elaborated and put his meaning beyond doubt.

"Androids can have and have had children."

Then the rest was drowned in a wave of gasps, whispers and

exclamations that swelled in a few seconds to a roar. The judge hammered and shouted in vain.

There was anger in the shouts. There was excitement, anxiety, incredulity, fear. Either the doctor was lying or he wasn't. If he was lying, he would suffer for it. People tricked by such a hoax are angry, vengeful people.

If he wasn't lying, everyone must re-evaluate his whole view of life. Everyone—human and android. The old religious questions would come up again. The question would be decided of whether Man, himself becoming extinct, had actually conquered life, instead of merely reaching a compromise with it. It would cease to matter whether any person was born or made.

There would be no more androids, only human beings. And Man would be master of creation.

VIII

The court sat again after a brief adjournment. The judge peered at Alison and at Dr. Smith, who was again on the stand.

"Mrs. Liffcom," he said, "would you care to take up your examination on the same point?"

"Certainly," said Alison. She addressed herself to Dr. Smith. "You say that androids can have children?"

This time there was silence except for the doctor's quiet voice. "Yes. There is, as may well be imagined, conflicting evidence on this. The evidence I propose to bring forward has frequently been discredited. The reaction when I first made this statement shows why. It is an important question on which everyone must have reached some conclusion. Possibly one merely believes what one is told."

As he went on, Alison cast a glance at Roderick. At first he was indifferent. He didn't believe it. Then he showed mild interest in what the doctor was saying. Eventually he became so excited that he could hardly sit still.

And Alison began to hope again.

"There is a psychologist in court," remarked the doctor mildly, "who may soon be asking me questions. I am not a psychologist any more than any other general practitioner, but before I mention particular cases, I must make this point. Every android grows up knowing he or she cannot have children. That is accepted in our civilization.

"I don't think it should be accepted. I'll tell you why."

No one interrupted him. He wasn't spectacular, but he wasted no time.

He mentioned the case of Betty Gordon Holbein, 178 years before. No one had heard of Betty Gordon Holbein. She was human, said the doctor. Prostrate with shock, she testified she had been raped by an android. The android concerned was lynched. In due course, Betty Holbein had a normal child.

"The records are available to everyone," said the doctor. "There was a lot of interest and indignation when the girl was raped, very little when she had her child. The suggestion that she had conceived after the incident was denied, without much publicity or belief, for even then it was *known* that androids were barren."

Roderick was on his feet. He looked at the judge, who nodded.

"Look, are you twisting this to make a legal case," he demanded, "or did this girl—"

"You cannot ask the witness if he is perjuring himself," remarked the judge reprovingly.

"I don't give a damn about perjury!" Roderick exclaimed. "I just want to know if this is true!"

It was all very irregular; but Alison knew he might explode any moment and swear at the doctor and the judge. She didn't want that. So her eyes met his and she said levelly: "It's true, Roderick."

Roderick sat down.

"Now to get a true picture," the doctor continued, "we must remember that millions of androids were being tested, and mating among themselves, and even having irregular liaisons with humans—and no conception took place. Or did it?"

A little over a century ago, an android girl had been found in a wood, alive, but only just. Around her there were marks of many feet. She had been mutilated. Though she lived, she was never quite sane after that.

But she also had a child.

Roderick rose again, frowning. "I don't understand," he said. "If this is true, why is it not known?"

The judge was going to intervene, but Roderick went on quickly, "The doctor and I are professional men. I can ask him for a professional opinion, surely? Well, Doctor?"

"Because it has always been possible to disbelieve what one has becided to disbelieve. In this case, that nameless woman was mutilated so that the navel mark would be removed. There was a record of her fingerprints as those of an android. But it was authoritatively stated that there must have been a mistake and that, by having a child, the woman had thus been proved to be human."

A century and a half ago, Winnie—androids had begun to have at least a first name by this time—had a child and it was again decided that this girl, who had been a laundry maid, must have been mixed up with an android while a baby and was in fact human.

A little dead baby was found buried in a garden and an android couple was actually in court over the matter. But since they were androids, it could obviously not be their child, and they were discharged.

Roderick jumped up again. "If you knew this," he asked Dr. Smith, "why keep it a secret until now?"

"Five years ago," said the doctor, "I wrote an article on the subject. I sent it to all the medical journals. Eventually one of the smaller publications printed it. I had half a dozen letters from people who were interested. Then nothing more.

"One must admit," he added, "that not one of the cases I have mentioned—as reported at the time—would be accepted as positive scientific proof that androids can reproduce. The facts were recorded for posterity by people who didn't believe them. But . . ."

"But," said Alison, a few minutes later, when the doctor had finished giving his evidence, "in view of this, it can hardly be stated that I *know* I cannot have a child. It may be unlikely; shall I call more medical evidence to show how unlikely conception is for the average human woman?"

Judge Collier said nothing, so she continued: "The present position, as anyone concerned with childbirth would tell you, is that few marriages produce children, but those that do produce a lot. People who *can* have children go on doing it, these days.

"Now I want to introduce a new point. It is not grounds for divorce among humans if the woman is barren and is not aware of it. It *is*, on the other hand, if she has an operation which makes it impossible for her to have children and she conceals the fact."

"I see what you are getting at," said the judge, "and it is most ingenious. Finish it, please."

"Having had no such operation," said Alison, "and being able to prove it, I understand that I can't be held, legally, to have known that I could never have children."

"To save reference to case histories," said the judge contentedly, "I can say here and now that the lady is right. It is for the jury to decide on the merits of the case, but Mrs. Liffcom may be said to have established—''

''I demand an adjournment,'' said Roderick.

There was a low murmur that gradually died out. Roderick and Alison were both on their feet, staring at each other across ten yards of space. The intensity of their feeling could be felt by everyone in the courtroom.

''Court adjourned until tomorrow,'' said the judge hastily.

IX

Almost every newspaper which mentioned the Liffcom case committed contempt of court. Perhaps the feeling was that no action could be taken against so many. All the newspapers went into the rights and wrongs of the affair as if they were giving evidence, too. Very little of the material was pro- or anti-android. It was, rather, for or against the evidence brought up.

Anyone could see, remarked one newspaper bluntly, that Alison Liffcom was nobody's fool. If a woman like that went to the trouble of defending a suit of any kind, she would dig up something good and play it to the limit. This was no aspersion on the morals or integrity of Mrs. Liffcom, for whom the newspaper had the keenest admiration. All she had to do was cast the faintest doubt on the truism that androids could not reproduce. She had done that.

But that, of course, said the paper decisively, didn't mean that androids *could*.

Another newspaper took it from there. Just as good a case, it remarked, could have been made out for spiritualism, telepathy, possession, the existence of werewolves... Dr. Smith, who was undoubtedly sincere, had been misled by a few mistakes. Obviously, when androids were human in all respects save one, *some* humans would be passed off or mistaken for androids and vice versa. Equally obvious, the mistake would only be discovered if and when conception occurred, as in the cases quoted by Dr. Smith.

A third paper even offered Alison a point to make in court if she liked. True enough, Dr. Smith had shown that such mistakes could occur. It was only necessary for Alison then to quote these cases and stress the possibility that the same thing might have happened to her. If the proof of android origin was not proof, the case would collapse.

Other papers, however, took the view that there might be something in the possibility that androids could reproduce. Why not? asked one. Androids weren't bloodless, inferior beings. One could keep things warm by holding them against the human body—or by building a fire. In the same way, children could be nurtured in a human body or in culture tanks. The results were identical. They must be identical if one could take them forty years later, give them rigorous tests, and tell one from the other only because the android was stamped "Made in U.S.A." and because his fingerprints were on file.

People had believed androids could not have children because they had been told androids never had. Now they were told androids *had* reproduced. Where was the difficulty? You believed you had finished your cigarettes until you took out the pack and saw there was one left. What did you do then—say you had finished them, therefore that what looked like a cigarette wasn't, and throw it away?

And almost all the newspapers, whatever their general view, asked the real, fundamental question as well.

That artificially made humans could conceive was credible, in theory. That they could not was also credible, in theory.

But why one in a million, one in five million, one in ten million? Even present-day humans could average one fertile marriage in six.

X

"If you have no objections," said Roderick politely—determined to be on his best behavior, thought Alison—"let's turn this into a court of inquiry. Let's say, if you like, that Alison has successfully defended the case on the grounds that she can't legally be said to have known she couldn't have a child. Forget the divorce. That's not the point."

"I thought it was," the judge objected, dazed.

"Anyone can see that what matters now," said Roderick impatiently, "is what Dr. Smith brought up. Let's get down to the question of whether there's any prospect of Alison having a baby."

"A courtroom is hardly the place to settle that," murmured Alison. But she felt the first warm breath of a glow of happiness she had thought she would never be able to experience again.

"Women always go from the general to the particular," Roderick retorted. "I don't mean the question of whether you *will* have children. I mean the question of whether it's really possible that you might."

The judge rapped decisively. "I have been too lenient. I insist on having a certain amount of order in my own court. Roderick Liffcom, do you withdraw your suit?"

"What does it matter? Anyway, if you must follow that line, we'd have to have a few straight questions and answers, like whether Alison still loves me."

The judge gasped.

"Do you?" demanded Roderick, glaring at Alison.

Alison felt as if her heart were going to explode. "If you want a straight answer," she said, "yes."

"Good," said Roderick with satisfaction. "Now we can go on from there."

He turned to glower at Judge Collier, who was trying to interrupt.

"Look here," Roderick demanded, "are you interested in getting at the truth?"

"Certainly, but—"

"So am I. Be quiet, then. I meant to keep my temper with you, but you're constantly getting in my hair. Alison, would you mind taking the stand?

There was no doubt that Roderick had personality.

With Alison on the stand, he turned to the jury. "I'll tell you what I have in mind," he told them in friendly fashion. "We all wonder why, if this thing's possible, it's happened so seldom. Unfortunately, to date there hasn't been any real admission that it is possible, so I didn't know. I never had a chance to work on it. Now I have. What I want to know is, if androids can have children, what prevents them from doing so?"

He reached out absent-mindedly, without looking around, and squeezed Alison's shoulder. "We've got Alison here," Roderick went on. "Let's find out, if we can, shall we, what would stop her from having children?"

Alison was glad she was sitting down. Her knees felt so weak that she knew they wouldn't support her. Did she have Roderick back or didn't she? Could she really have a baby? *Roderick's* baby? The court swam dizzily in front of her eyes.

Only gradually did she become aware of Roderick's voice asking anxiously if she was all right, Roderick bending over her, Roderick's arm behind her back, supporting her.

"Yes," she said faintly. "I'm sorry, Roderick, I'll help you all I can, but do you think there's really very much chance?"

"I'm a psychologist," he reminded her quietly, "and since you've never seen me at work, there's no harm in telling you I'm pretty good. Maybe we won't work this out here in half an hour, but we'll get through it in the next sixty years."

Alison didn't forget where she was, but everything was so crazy that a little more wouldn't hurt. She reached up and drew his lips down to hers.

XI

"What I'm looking for must be in the life of every android, male and female," said Roderick. "I don't expect to find it right away. Just tell us, Alison, about any times when you were aware of distinction—when you were made aware that you were an android, not a human. Start as early as you like.

"And," he added with a sudden, unexpected grin, "please address your remarks to the judge. Let's keep this as impersonal as we can."

Alison composed her mind for the job. She didn't really want to look back. She wanted to look into the new, marvelous future. But she forced herself to begin.

"I grew up in the New York Android Creche," she said. "There was no distinction there. Some of the children thought there was. Sometimes I heard older children talking about how much better off they would be if they were humans. But twice when there was overcrowding in the creche and plenty of room at the orphanage for human children, I was moved to the orphanage. And there was absolutely no difference.

"In a creche, it's far more important to be able to sell yourself that it ever can be later. If you're attractive or appealing enough, someone looking for a child to adopt will notice you and you'll have a home and security and affection. I wasn't attractive or appealing. I stayed in the creche until I was nine. I saw so many couples looking for children, always taking away some child but never me, that I was sure I would stay there until I was too old to be adopted and then have to earn my living, always on my own.

"Then, one day, one of the sisters at the creche found me crying—I forget what I was crying about—and told me there was no need for me to cry about anything because I had brains and I was going to be a beauty, and what more could any girl want? I looked in the mirror, but I still seemed the same as ever. She must have known what she was talking about, though, for just a week later, a couple came and looked around the creche and picked me.''

Alison took a deep breath, and there was no acting about the tears in her eyes.

"Nobody who's never experienced it can appreciate what it is to have a home for the first time at the age of nine," she said. "To say I'd have died for my new parents doesn't tell half of it. Maybe this is something that misled Roderick. He knew that twice a month, at least, I go and see my folks. He must have thought they were my real parents, so he didn't ask if I was android."

She looked at Roderick for the first time since she started the story. He nodded.

"Go on, Alison," he said quietly. "You're doing fine."

"This isn't a hard world for androids," Alison insisted. "It's only very occasionally . . ."

She stopped, and Roderick had to prompt her. "Only very occasionally that what?"

But Alison wasn't with him. She was eleven years back in the past.

XII

Alison had known all about that awkward period when she would cease to be a child and become a woman. But she had never quite realized how rapid it would be, and how it would seem even more rapid, so that it was over before she was ready for it to start.

She wasn't sleeping well, but she was so healthy and had such reserves of strength that it didn't show, and for once her adopted parents failed her. Though Alison would never admit that, it would have been so much easier if Susan had talked with her, and Roger, without saying a word, had indicated in his manner that he knew what was going on.

One day she was out walking, trying to tire herself for sleep later, and ran into a group of youths her own age in the woods. She knew one of them slightly, Bob Thomson, and she knew that their apparent leader, as tall as a man at fifteen, was Harry Hewitt. She didn't know whether any of them were androids or not—the question had never occurred to her. And it didn't seem of any immediate interest or importance that she was an android, either, as she passed through them and some of them whistled, and involuntarily, completely aware of their eyes on her, she reddened.

She saw Bob Thomson whisper to Harry Hewitt and Hewitt burst out: "Android, eh? *Android!* That's fine!" He stepped in front of her and barred her path. "What a pretty android," he said loudly, playing to his gallery. "I've seen you before, but I thought you were just a girl. Take off your blouse, android."

There was a startled movement in the group, and someone nudged Hewitt.

"It's all right," he said. "She's an android. No real parents, only people who have taken her in to pretend they can have kids."

Alison looked from side to side like a cornered animal.

"Humans can do anything they like with androids," Hewitt told his more timorous companions. "Don't you know that?" He turned back to Alison. "But we must be sure she is an android. Hold her, Butch."

Alison was grasped firmly by the hips, which had so recently stopped being boyish and swelled alarmingly. She kicked and struggled, her heart threatening to burst, but Butch, whoever he was, was strong. Two other boys held her arms. Carefully, to a chorus of nervous, excited sniggers, Hewitt parted her blouse and skirt a narrow slit and peered at her navel.

"Made in U.S.A.," he said with satisfaction. "It's all right, then."

In contrast to his previous cautious, decorous manner, he tore the blouse out of her waistband and ripped it off. Alison's knees sagged as someone behind her began to fumble with her brassiere.

"No, no!" Hewitt exclaimed in mock horror. "Mustn't do that until she says you can. Even androids have rights. Or at least, if they haven't, we should be polite and pretend they have. Android, say we can do whatever we like with you."

"No!" cried Alison.

"That's too bad. Shift your grip a bit, Butch."

The rough hands went up around her ribs, rasping her soft skin.

Alison struggled and twisted wildly.

"Keep still," said Hewitt. He spoke very quietly, but there was savage joy in his face. Slowly and carefully, he loosened Alison's belt and eased her skirt and the white trunks under it down to the pit of her stomach. Then he took out a heavy clasp knife, opened it and set the point neatly in the center of her belly. Alison drew in her stomach; the knife point followed, indenting the flesh.

"Say we can do whatever we like with you, android."

The knife pricked deeper. A tiny drop of crimson came from under it and ran slowly down to Alison's skirt. Her nerve broke.

"You can do whatever you like with me!" she screamed.

Her brassiere came loose and fluttered to the ground. Hewitt's knife cut her belt and her skirt began to slip over her hips. Butch's hands went down to her waist again, biting into it cruelly. From behind, a hand tentatively touched her breast and another clutched her shoulder. One at a time, her feet were raised and the shoes taken off them and thrown in the bushes.

But someone else had heard Alison's scream. Long after she had thought no one would come, someone did.

"Hell," said Hewitt as one of his companions shouted and pointed, "something always spoils everything. Beat it, boys."

They were gone. Alison clutched her skirt and looked behind her thankfully. A man and a woman were only a few yards from her. The woman was young and heavy with child. Humans, both of them. She opened her mouth to thank them, to explain, to weep.

But they were looking at her as if she were a crushed beetle of some kind.

"Android, of course," said the man disgustedly. "Dirty little beast."

"Hardly more than a child," the woman said, "and already at this."

"I think I'll give her a good hiding," the man went on. "Won't do any good, I suppose, but . . ."

Alison burst into tears and darted among the bushes. She didn't wait to see whether the man started after her. Branches and thorns tore her skin. Her skirt dropped and tripped her. She flew headlong, flinched away from a thorny bush, slammed hard into a tree trunk, and waited on the ground, sick and breathless, for the man to beat her.

Her legs and shoulders were covered with long scratches and a wiry branch had lashed her ribs like a whip, leaving a long weal. But that didn't matter. A twisted root was digging into her side—that, too, didn't matter. Nothing mattered. Why had no one told her she was an inferior being? Somehow she had known; she had always known. But no one had ever *shown* her before.

She realized afterward why the man and the woman, who must have seen or guessed what really happened, had spoken as they did. They had, or were going to have, children. They hated all androids. Androids were unnecessary, their enemies, and the enemies of children.

But at that time she merely waited helpless, incapable of thought. The man would come and beat her, Susan and Roger would turn her away, and she would never know happiness again.

XIII

"My parents never knew about that," said Alison. "I hid in the bushes until it was dark, and then went straight home. I climbed into my bedroom from the outhouse and pretended later that I'd been there for hours."

"Why didn't you tell anyone?" Roderick asked.

Alison shrugged. "It was a small incident that concerned me alone. I knew, once I'd had time to think, that my adopted parents would be upset and angry, but not at me. I thought I'd better keep it to myself. I wasn't hurt and none of it matters when you look back on it, does it?"

"How about the man who was going to give you a good hiding?"

"I never saw him again. It was two years later when I got my first punishment."

"Just a minute," said Roderick. "You said that even then you knew you were an inferior being—you had always known, but this was the first time anyone showed you. How had you known? Who or what told you? When? Where?"

Alison tried. They could see her try. But she had to say: "I don't know."

"All right," said Roderick, as if it weren't important. "What was this that happened two years later?"

"Perhaps I am giving too much significance to these incidents," Alison remarked apologetically. "Certainly they happened. But when I say 'two years passed,' perhaps I'm not making it clear that in those two years hardly anything happened, hardly anything was said or done, to remind me I was an android and not a human being.

"When I was about sixteen or seventeen, I suddenly developed a talent for tennis. I had played since I was quite young, but just as front-rank players run in and out of form, I improved quite unexpectedly. I joined a new club. I was picked for an important match. I was in singles, mixed and women's doubles. I did well, but that's not the point.

"After the match, my doubles partner told me I was wanted in the locker room. There was something strange about the way she told me, but I couldn't place it. I wondered if I'd broken some rule, failed to check with someone, played in the wrong match, or forgotten to bow three times to the east—you know what these doubts are like."

"No, we don't," said Judge Collier. "We know nothing, remember? Tell us."

Unexpectedly, he got an approving nod from the unpredictable Roderick.

XIV

Alison smiled uncertainly as she followed Veronica. She wasn't nervous or sensitive as a rule; she seldom felt apprehension. She was curious, naturally, and even wilder possibilities suggested themselves. Had she been mistaken for someone else? Had someone stolen something and they thought she'd done it? Had someone inspected her racket and found it was an inch too wide?

The whole team was waiting in the locker room. It looked serious, especially when she saw their expressions. It still didn't occur to her that the fact that she was an android could have anything to do with it. Only once in her life had there been any real indication that in some way androids were inferior beings.

But that was what it was. Bob Walton, the captain of the

team, said gravely that their opponents, well beaten, had accused them of recruiting star androids to help them.

Alison laughed. "That's a new one. I've heard some peculiar excuses. Made them myself, too—the light was bad, the umpire was crazy, I had a stone in my shoe, people were moving about, the net was too high. But never 'You fielded androids against us.' Androids are just ordinary people—good and bad tennis players. The open-singles champion is an android, but the number-one woman is human. You know that as well as I do. Might as well complain because you're beaten by tall people, or short people, or people with long arms."

Everyone had relaxed.

"Sorry, Alison," said Walton. "It's just that none of us knew you *weren't* an android."

Alison frowned. "What's all this? I'm an android, sure. I didn't say so only because nobody asked me."

"We took it for granted," said Walton stiffly, "that you would know . . . as, of course, you did. There are no androids competing in the Athenian League. We try to keep one group, at least, clean."

He looked at the other two men in the team and inclined his head. Without a word they left the room, all three of them.

Alison, left with the other three girls, one of whom she had kept out of the team, looked exasperated.

"This is nonsense," she said. "If you like to run an all-human league, that's all right as far as I'm concerned, but you should put up notices to avoid misunderstanding. I didn't know you were—"

"Whether you knew or not is beside the point," said Veronica coldly—the same Veronica who had laughed and talked and won a match with Alison only a few minutes before. "We're going to make sure you never forget."

They closed in on her. It was to be a fight, apparently. Alison didn't mind. She jabbed Veronica in the ribs and sent her gasping across the room. She expected them to tear her clothes, thinking it would be conventional in dealing with android girls. but it was quite different from the scene in the bushes. This was clean and sporting. The men had left, very properly, and instead of half a dozen youths with a knife against a terrified child, it was only three girls to one.

Alison fought hard, but fair. She guessed that, if she didn't fight clean, it would be more ammunition for the android-haters. To do them justice, the other girls were clean, too. They didn't mind hurting her, but they didn't go for her face, use their nails or yank her hair.

Alison gave a good account of herself, but other things being equal, three will always overcome one. She was turned on her face on the floor. One of the girls sat on her legs and one on her shoulders while the third beat the seat of her shorts with a firmly swung racket.

It was no joke. Alison wouldn't have made a sound if it had been far worse, but when they let her go, she was feeling sorry for herself. They left her alone in the room.

She picked herself up and dusted herself off. The floor was clean and the mirror in one corner showed that she looked all right. In fact, she looked considerably better than the three girls who had beaten her.

Still angry, she was able to grin philosophically at the thought that she could beat them all in a beauty contest and at tennis. She could tell herself, if she liked, that they were all jealous of her. It was probably at least partly true.

Her feelings were hurt, but there was no other damage. She could even see their point of view.

XV

"What *was* their point of view?" asked Roderick.

"Well, they were human and they were snobs. They'd even have admitted they were snobs, if you put the question the right way. It was a private club—"

"And it was quite reasonable," suggested Roderick softly, "that they should exclude androids, who are inferior beings."

"No, not quite that," Alison protested, laughing. "I don't really believe . . ."

She stopped.

"Just sometimes?" Roderick persisted. "Or just one part of you, while the other knows quite well an android is as good as a human?"

Alison shivered suddenly. "You know, I have a curious feeling, as if I were being trapped into something."

"That's how people always feel," said Roderick, "just before they decide they needn't be terrified any more of spiders or whatever it was they feared."

The court was very quiet. There was something about Roderick's professional competence and Alison's determination to cooperate that made any kind of interruption out of the question.

"There's very little more I can say about this," said Alison. "I took a job, not because I had to, but because I wanted to. It was with an advertising agency. They knew I was an android. They paid me exactly what they paid anyone else. When I did well, they gave me a raise."

"But then I noticed something—I never got any credit for anything. When I had an idea, somehow it was always possible to give the credit to someone else. Soon there was a very curious situation. I had a very junior position, I had little or no standing, but I did responsible work and I was paid well for it.

"I went to another agency and it was quite different. Again, they knew I was an android, but no one seemed remotely interested. When I did well, I was promoted. When I did badly on my job, my chief swore at me and called me a fool and an incompetent and an empty-headed glamour girl and a lot of things I'd rather not repeat here.

"But it never seemed to occur to him to call me a dirty android. I don't think he was an android himself, either.

"I joined a dramatic society, but again I chose the wrong club. They didn't mind at all that I was an android. They didn't keep me in small parts. But it was perfectly natural that the three human girls in the cast shouldn't want to use the same dressing room as another android girl in the show and I did. When we were at small places, she and I had to change in the wings.

"There were scores of other little incidents of the same kind. They multiplied as I grew older—not because differentiation was getting worse, but because I was moving in higher society. In places where it's held against you that you didn't go to Harvard or Yale, naturally it's a disadvantage if you're an android, besides.

"Then a law was passed and it was no longer necessary to admit being an android. I don't know what the Athenian Tennis League did about that. I'd come to Everton then and hardly anyone knew I was an android. And the plain fact, despite everything I've said, is that hardly anyone cared. There are so many androids, so many humans. You may find yourself the only android in a group—or the only human.

"Then I met Roderick."

"There," said Roderick, "I think we can stop." He turned to the judge. "I'm withdrawing my suit, of course. I think I made that clear quite a while ago."

He gave Alison his arm. "Come on, sweetheart, let's go."

The roar burst out again. It must have been both one of the noisiest and one of the quietest trials on record. The judge, dignity forgotten, was standing up, hopping from one foot to the other in impatience and vexation.

"You can't go like that!" he shrieked. "We haven't finished . . . we don't know . . ."

"I've gone as far as I can here," said Roderick. He hesitated as the roar grew. "All right," he went on, raising his voice. "But you don't explain people to themselves. Any little quirks that make them do funny things, or not do normal things, you get them gradually to explain to you, and to themselves."

He searched in his pockets and pulled out a key ring. "Go and wait in the car, honey," he said, and told Alison where it was. She went, dazed.

"I'll have to keep the papers from her for a day or two," Roderick went on, almost to himself. "After that, it won't matter." He turned his attention to the court. "All right, then, listen. If I'm right, I've found something that's been under everyone's nose for two hundred years and has never been seen before. I don't say I found it in five minutes. I've been working it out for the last twenty-four hours, with the help of quite a few records of android patients.

"Will you listen?" he yelled as the excited chatter increased. "I don't want to tell you this. I want to go home with Alison. You've seen her. Wouldn't you want to?"

The court gradually settled.

"Let's consider human sterility for a moment," said Roderick. "As you might imagine, some of it's medical and some psychological. As a psychologist, I've cured people of so-called barrenness—and when I did, of course, it wasn't sterility at all, but a neurosis. These people didn't and don't have children because, owing to some unconscious conclusion they've reached, they don't want them, feel they shouldn't have them, or are certain they can't have them.

"But that's only some. Others come to me and, in consultation with a specialist in that line, I find there's nothing psychological about it whatever.

"I have an idea, now, that *all* androids are psychologically sterile. Sterility has eaten into the cycle of human reproduction, but how should it touch the androids? If one android can reproduce, they all can. Unless they, like these humans I've cured, have reached unconscious conclusions to the effect that androids can't or shouldn't or mustn't have children.

"And we know they nearly all have."

His voice suddenly dropped, and when Roderick spoke quietly, he was emphasizing points and people listened. There was no murmuring now.

"I think if you were to run a survey and find who now is continuing to deny—passionately, honestly, sincerely—that androids can reproduce, you'd find the most passionate, honest and sincere are androids. If you looked into the past, I think you'd find the same thing. Wasn't it significant that it had to be a *human* doctor who declared publicly that androids weren't sterile?

"Into every android is built the psychological axiom that an android must be inferior to a human to survive. That's the answer. Androids don't come to me to be cured of this because they don't *want* to be cured of it. They know it's essential to them. With the more aware part of their brains, they may know exactly the opposite, but that doesn't count when it comes to things like this.

"And long ago, without knowing it, androids picked on this. Androids could not be a menace if they couldn't reproduce. Androids would be allowed to exist if they couldn't reproduce. Androids would be duly inferior if they couldn't reproduce. Androids could compete with humans in other things if they couldn't reproduce."

He knew he was right as he looked around the court. For once, almost at a glance, it was possible to tell humans from androids. Half the people in the court were interested, bored, amused, indifferent, thoughtful—the humans. The other half were angry, frightened, ashamed, apathetic, resentful, wildly excited, or in tears . . . for Roderick was tearing at the very foundation of their world.

"I have real hopes for Alison," he remarked mildly, "because she brought in Dr. Smith. See what that means? Not one android in a thousand could have done it. She must love me a lot . . . but that's none of your business."

He went the way Alison had gone. No one tried to stop him this time. At the door, he paused.

"When the first acknowledged android children are born," he observed, "it'll mean that regardless of the trials or disasters mankind still has to face, the *human* race won't die out. Because . . . I think we might all chew a little on this point . . . the children of androids can't be android, can they?"

XVII

Roderick drove. Alison usually did when they were out in a car together, but there was an unspoken agreement that Roderick would have to take charge of almost everything for a while.

"We both won," she said happily. "At least, we will have when little Roderick arrives."

"Do you believe he will?" asked Roderick, in his professional, neutral tone.

"Not quite. I wonder what you said in the court. I suppose I'm not to try to find out?"

"Find out if you like. But do it from yourself. From what's in you. I'll help."

"I think it must be something to do with Dr. Smith."

"Oh? Why?"

"Because I had the most peculiar feeling when I remembered hearing about him and the idea that androids could have children. Like when Hewitt had his knife in my stomach, only as if . . ."

She laughed nervously, uncomfortably. "As if I were holding it myself, and had to cut something out, but couldn't do it without killing myself. Yet I had a sort of idea I could cut it out, if I tried hard enough and long enough, and *not* kill myself."

Roderick turned the corner into their street. "This is a little unprofessional," he said, the exhilaration in his voice ill-concealed, "but I don't think it'll do any harm with you, Alison. There is going to be a little Roderick. I didn't decide it. *You* decided it. And it won't kill you. And—God, look at that!"

Cameras clicked like grasshoppers as Roderick Liffcom carried his bride across the threshold. The photographers hadn't had to follow them, for they knew where the Liffcoms were going. Scores of plates were exposed. The Liffcoms were news. The name of Liffcom was known to almost everyone.

Roderick was big and strong enough to treat his wife's 115 pounds with contempt, but there was no contempt in the way he held her. He carried here as if she were made of crystal which the faintest jar would shatter. One could see at a glance that he could have carried any girl he liked over the threshold.

Alison nestled in his arms like a kitten, eyes half-closed with rapture, arms about Roderick's neck. One could see at a glance she could have been carried over the threshold by any man she liked.

As they went in, it was the beginning of a story. But let's be different and call it the end.

THE ELECTRIC ANT

Phillip K. Dick

"Things are seldom what they seem," sings Little Buttercup in Gilbert & Sullivan's H.M.S. Pinafore, *and in the surreal and hallucinatory science fiction of Philip K. Dick that "seldom" becomes a "never." Reality, to Dick, is nothing more than a series of constantly shifting surfaces that part occasionally to reveal mysteries beyond mysteries. One aspect of reality that runs through many of Dick's stories involves androids, those lifelike imitations of humanity that our troubled future is apt to spawn. In a world where artificial entities mingle indistinguishably with true human beings, how can one tell the android from the human? How can you know whether you yourself are real?*

At four fifteen in the afternoon, T.S.T., Garson Poole woke up in his hospital bed, knew that he lay in a hospital bed in a three-bed ward and realized in addition two things: that he no longer had a right hand and that he felt no pain.

They have given me a strong analgesic, he said to himself as he stared at the far wall with its window showing downtown New York. Webs in which vehicles and peds darted and wheeled glimmered in the late-afternoon sun, and the brilliance of the aging light pleased him. It's not yet out, he thought. And neither am I.

A fone lay on the table beside his bed; he hesitated, then picked it up and dialed for an outside line. A moment later he was faced by Louis Danceman, in charge of Tri-Plan's activities while he, Garson Poole, was elsewhere.

"Thank god you're alive," Danceman said, seeing him; his big, fleshy face with its moon's surface of pockmarks flattened with relief. "I've been calling all—"

"I just don't have a right hand," Poole said.

"But you'll be okay. I mean, they can graft another one on."

"How long have I been here?" Poole said. He wondered where the nurses and doctors had gone to; why weren't they clucking and fussing about him making a call?

"Four days," Danceman said. "Everything here at the plant is going splunkishly. In fact we've splunked orders from three separate police systems, all here on Terra. Two in Ohio, one in Wyoming. Good solid orders, with one third in advance and the usual three-year lease-option."

"Come and get me out of here," Poole said.

"I can't get you out until the new hand—"

"I'll have it done later." He wanted desperately to get back to familiar surroundings; memory of the mercantile squib looming grotesquely on the pilot screen careened at the back of his mind; if he shut his eyes he felt himself back in his damaged craft as it plunged from one vehicle to another, piling up enormous damage as it went. The kinetic sensations . . . he winced, recalling them. I guess I'm lucky, he said to himself.

"Is Sarah Benton there with you?" Danceman asked.

"No." Of course; his personal secretary—if only for job considerations—would be hovering close by, mothering him in her jejune, infantile way. All heavy-set women like to mother people, he thought. And they're dangerous; if they fall on you they can kill you. ''Maybe that's what happened to me,'' he said aloud. ''Maybe Sarah fell on my squib.''

''No, no; a tie rod in the steering fin of your squib split apart during the rush-hour traffic and you—''

''I remember.'' He turned in his bed as the door of the ward opened; a white-clad doctor and two blue-clad nurses appeared, making their way toward his bed. ''I'll talk to you later,'' Poole said, and hung up the fone. He took a deep, expectant breath.

''You shouldn't be foning quite so soon,'' the doctor said as he studied his chart. ''Mr. Garson Poole, owner of Tri-Plan Electronics. Maker of random ident darts that track their prey for a circle-radius of a thousand miles, responding to unique enceph wave patterns. You're a successful man, Mr. Poole. But, Mr. Poole, you're not a man. You're an electric ant.''

''Christ,'' Poole said, stunned.

''So we can't really treat you here, now that we've found out. We knew, of course, as soon as we examined your injured right hand; we saw the electronic components and then we made torso X rays and of course they bore out our hypothesis.''

''What,'' Poole said, ''is an 'electric ant'?'' But he knew; he could decipher the term.

A nurse said, ''An organic robot.''

''I see,'' Poole said. Frigid perspiration rose to the surface of his skin, across all his body.

''You didn't know,'' the doctor said.

''No.'' Poole shook his head.

The doctor said, ''We get an electric ant every week or so. Either brought in here from a squib accident—like yourself—or one seeking voluntary admission . . . one who, like yourself, has never been told, who has functioned alongside humans, believing himself—itself—human. As to your hand—'' He paused.

''Forget my hand,'' Poole said savagely.

''Be calm.'' The doctor leaned over him, peered acutely

down into Poole's face. "We'll have a hospital boat convey you over to a service facility where repairs, or replacement, on your hand can be made at a reasonable expense, either to yourself, if you're self-owned, or to your owners, if such there are. In any case you'll be back at your desk at Tri-Plan, functioning just as before."

"Except," Poole said, "now I know." He wondered if Danceman or Sarah or any of the others at the office knew. Had they—or one of them—purchased him? Designed him? A figurehead, he said to himself; that's all I've been. I must never really have run the company; it was a delusion implanted in me when I was made . . . along with the delusion that I am human and alive.

"Before you leave for the repair facility," the doctor said, "could you kindly settle your bill at the front desk?"

Poole said acidly, "How can there be a bill if you don't treat ants here?"

"For our services," the nurse said. "Up until the point we knew."

"Bill me," Poole said, with furious, impotent anger. "Bill my firm." With massive effort he managed to sit up; his head swimming, he stepped haltingly from the bed and onto the floor. "I'll be glad to leave here," he said as he rose to a standing position. "And thank you for your humane attention."

"Thank you, too, Mr. Poole," the doctor said. "Or rather I should say just Poole."

At the repair facility he had his missing hand replaced.

It proved fascinating, the hand; he examined it for a long time before he let the technicians install it. On the surface it appeared organic—in fact, on the surface it was. Natural skin covered natural flesh, and true blood filled the veins and capillaries. But, beneath that, wires and circuits, miniaturized components, gleamed . . . looking deep into the wrist he saw surge gates, motors, multi-stage valves, all very small. Intricate. And—the hand cost forty frogs. A week's salary, insofar as he drew it from the company payroll.

"Is that guaranteed?" he asked the technicians as they refused the "bone" section of the hand to the balance of his body.

"Ninety days, parts and labor," one of the technicians said. "Unless subjected to unusual or intentional abuse."

"That sounds vaguely suggestive," Poole said.

The technician, a man—all of them were men—said, regarding him keenly, "You've been posing?"

"Unintentionally," Poole said.

"And now it's intentional?"

Poole said, "Exactly."

"Do you know why you've never guessed? There must have been signs . . . clickings and whirrings from inside you, now and then. You never guessed because you were programmed not to notice. You'll now have the same difficulty finding out why you were built and for whom you've been operating."

"A slave," Poole said. "A mechanical slave."

"You've had fun."

"I've lived a good life," Poole said. "I've worked hard."

He paid the facility its forty frogs, flexed his new fingers, tested them by picking up various objects such as coins, then departed. Ten minutes later he was aboard a public carrier, on him way home. It had been quite a day.

At home, in his one-room apartment, he poured himself a shot of Jack Daniels Purple Label—sixty years old—and sat sipping it, meanwhile gazing through his sole window at the building on the opposite side of the street. Shall I go to the office? he asked himself. If so, why? If not, why? Choose one. Christ, he thought, it undermines you, knowing this. I'm a freak, he realized. An inanimate object mimicking an animate one. But—

he felt alive. Yet... he felt differently, now. About himself. Hence about everyone, especially Danceman and Sarah, everyone at Tri-Plan.

I think I'll kill myself, he said to himself. But I'm probably programmed not to do that; it would be a costly waste which my owner would have to absorb. And he wouldn't want to.

Programmed. In me somewhere, he thought, there is a matrix fitted in place, a grid screen that cuts me off from certain thoughts, certain actions. And forces me into others. I am not free. I never was, but now I know it; that makes it different.

Turning his window to opaque, he snapped on the overhead light, carefully set about removing his clothing, piece by piece. He had watched carefully as the technicians at the repair facility had attached his new hand: he had a rather clear idea, now, of how his body had been assembled. Two major panels, one in each thigh; the technicians had removed the panels to check the circuit complexes beneath. If I'm programmed, he decided, the matrix probably can be found there.

The maze of circuitry baffled him. I need help, he said to himself. Let's see... what's the fone code for the class BBB computer we hire at the office?

He picked up the fone, dialed the computer at its permanent location in Boise, Idaho.

"Use of the computer is prorated at a five-frogs-per-minute basis," a mechanical voice from the fone said. "Please hold your mastercreditchargeplate before the screen."

He did so.

"At the sound of the buzzer you will be connected with the computer," the voice continued. "Please query it as rapidly as possible, taking into account the fact that its answer will be given in terms of a microsecond while your query will—"
He turned the sound down, then. But quickly turned it up as the blank audio input of the computer appeared on the screen.

At this moment the computer had become a giant ear, listening to him—as well as fifty thousand other queriers throughout Terra.

"Scan me visually," he instructed the computer. "And tell me where I will find the programming mechanism which controls my thoughts and behavior." He waited. On the fone's screen a great active eye, multilensed, peered at him; he displayed himself for it, there in his one-room apartment.

The computer said, "Remove your chest panel. Apply pressure at your breastbone and then ease outward."

He did so. A section of his chest came off; dizzily, he set it down on the floor.

"I can distinguish control modules," the computer said, "but I can't tell which—" It paused as its eye roved about on the fone screen. "I distinguish a roll of punched tape mounted above your heart mechanism. Do you see it?" Poole craned his neck, peered. He saw it, too. "I will have to sign off," the computer said. "After I have examined the data available to me I will contact you and give you an answer. Good day." The screen died out.

I'll yank the tape out of me, Poole said to himself. Tiny . . . no larger than two spools of thread, with a scanner mounted between the delivery drum and the take-up drum. He could not see any sign of motion; the spools seemed inert. They must cut in as override, he reflected, when specific situations occur. Override to my encephalic processes. And they've been doing it all my life.

He reached down, touched the delivery drum. All I have to do is tear this out, he thought, and—

The fone screen relit. "Mastercreditchargeplate number 3-BNX-882-HQR446-T," the computer's voice came. "This is BBR-307DR recontacting you in response to your query of sixteen seconds lapse, November 4, 1992. The punched tape roll above your heart mechanism is not a programming turret but is in fact a reality-supply construct. All sense stimuli received by your central neurological system emanate from that unit and tampering with it would be risky if not terminal.'' It added, ''You appear to have no programming circuit. Query answered. Good day.'' It flicked off.

Poole, standing naked before the fone screen, touched the tape drum once again, with calculated, enormous caution. I see, he thought wildly. Or do I see? This unit—

If I cut the tape, he realized, my world will disappear. Reality will continue for others, but not for me. Because my reality, my universe, is coming to me from this minuscule unit. Fed into the scanner and then into my central nervous system as it snailishly unwinds.

It has been unwinding for years, he decided.

Getting his clothes, he redressed, seated himself in his big armchair—a luxury imported into his apartment from Tri-Plan's main offices—and lit a tobacco cigarette. His hands shook as he laid down his initialed lighter; leaning back, he blew smoke before himself, creating a nimbus of gray.

I have to go slowly, he said to himself. What am I trying to do? Bypass my programming? But the computer found no programming circuit. Do I want to interfere with the reality tape? And if so, *why*?

Because, he thought, if I control that, I control reality. At least so far as I'm concerned. My subjective reality . . . but that's all there is. Objective reality is a synthetic construct, dealing with a hypothetical universalization of a multitude of subjective realities.

My universe is lying within my fingers, he realized. If I can just figure out how the damn thing works. All I set out to do originally was to search for and locate my programming circuit so I could gain true homeostatic functioning: control of myself. But with this—

With this he did not merely gain control of himself; he gained control over everything.

And this sets me apart from every human who ever lived and died, he thought somberly.

Going over to the fone, he dialed his office. When he had Danceman on the screen he said briskly, "I want you to send a complete set of microtools and enlarging screen over to my apartment. I have some microcircuitry to work on." Then he broke the connection, not wanting to discuss it.

A half-hour later a knock sounded on his door. When he opened up he found himself facing one of the shop foremen, loaded down with microtools of every sort. "You didn't say exactly what you wanted," the foreman said, entering the apartment. "So Mr. Danceman had me bring everything."

"And the enlarging-lens system?"

"In the truck, up on the roof."

Maybe what I want to do, Poole thought, is die. He lit a cigarette, stood smoking and waiting as the shop foreman lugged the heavy enlarging screen, with its power supply and control panel, into the apartment. This is suicide, what I'm doing here. He shuddered.

"Anything wrong, Mr. Poole?" the shop foreman said as he rose to his feet, relieved of the burden of the enlarging-lens system. "You must still be rickety on your pins from your accident."

"Yes," Poole said quietly. He stood tautly waiting until the foreman left.

Under the enlarging-lens system the plastic tape assumed a new shape: a wide track along which hundreds of thousands of punch-holes worked their way. I thought so, Poole thought. Not recorded as charges on a ferrous oxide layer, but actually punched-free slots.

Under the lens the strip of tape visibly oozed forward. Very slowly, but it did, at uniform velocity, move in the direction of the scanner.

The way I figure it, he thought, is that the punched holes are *on* gates. It functions like a player piano: solid is no, punch-hole is yes. How can I test this?

Obviously by filling in a number of the holes.

He measured the amount of tape left on the delivery spool, calculated—at great effort—the velocity of the tape's movement, and then came up with a figure. If he altered the tape visible at the in-going edge of the scanner, five to seven hours would pass before that particular time period arrived. He would in effect be painting out stimuli due a few hours from now.

With a microbrush he swabbed a large—relatively large— section of tape with opaque varnish . . . obtained from the supply kit accompanying the microtools. I have smeared out stimuli for about half an hour, he pondered. Have covered at least a thousand punches.

It would be interesting to see what change, if any, overcame his environment, six hours from now.

Five and a half hours later he sat at Krackter's, a superb bar in Manhattan, having a drink with Danceman.

"You look bad," said Danceman.

"I am bad," Poole said. He finished his drink, a Scotch sour, and ordered another.

"From the accident?"

"In a sense, yes."

Danceman said, "Is it—something you found out about yourself?"

Raising his head, Poole eyed him in the murky light of the bar. "Then you know."

"I know," Danceman said, "that I should call you 'Poole'

instead of 'Mr. Poole.' But I prefer the latter, and will continue to do so.''

"How long have you known?" Poole said.

"Since you took over the firm. I was told that the actual owners of Tri-Plan, who are located in the Prox System, wanted Tri-Plan run by an electronic ant whom they could control. They wanted a brilliant and forceful—"

"The real owners?" This was the first he had heard about that. "We have two thousand stockholders. Scattered everywhere."

"Marvis Bey and her husband Ernan, on Prox 4, control fifty-one percent of the voting stock. This has been true from the start."

"Why didn't I know?"

"I was told not to tell you. You were to think that you yourself made all company policy. With my help. But actually I was feeding you what the Beys fed to me."

"I'm a figurehead," Poole said.

"In a sense, yes." Danceman nodded. "But you'll always be 'Mr. Poole' to me."

A section of the far wall vanished. And with it, several people at tables nearby. And—

Through the big glass side of the bar, the skyline of New York City flickered out of existence.

Seeing his face, Danceman said, "What is it?"

Poole said hoarsely, "Look around. Do you see any changes?"

After looking around the room, Danceman said, "No. What like?"

"You still see the skyline?"

"Sure. Smoggy as it is. The lights wink—"

"Now I know," Poole said. He had been right; every punch-hole covered up meant the disappearance of some object in the reality world. Standing, he said, "I'll see you later, Danceman. I have to get back to my apartment; there's some work I'm doing. Good night." He strode from the bar and out onto the street, searching for a cab.

No cabs.

Those too, he thought. I wonder what else I painted over. Prostitutes? Flowers? Prisons?

There, in the bar's parking lot, Danceman's squib. I'll take that, he decided. There are still cabs in Danceman's world; he can get one later. Anyhow it's a company car, and I hold a copy of the key.

Presently he was in the air, turning toward his apartment.

New York City had not returned. To the left and right vehicles and buildings, streets, ped-runners, signs . . . and in the center nothing. How can I fly into that? he asked himself. I'd disappear.

Or would I? He flew toward the nothingness.

Smoking one cigarette after another, he flew in a circle for fifteen minutes . . . and then, soundlessly, New York reappeared. He could finish his trip. He stubbed out his cigarette (a waste of something so valuable) and shot off in the direction of his apartment.

If I insert a narrow opaque strip, he pondered as he unlocked his apartment door, I can—

His thoughts ceased. Someone sat in his living room chair, watching a captain kirk on the TV. "Sarah," he said, nettled.

She rose, well-padded but graceful. "You weren't at the hospital, so I came here. I still have that key you gave me back in March after we had that awful argument. Oh . . . you look so depressed." She came up to him, peeped into his face anxiously. "Does your injury hurt that badly?"

"It's not that." He removed his coat, tie, shirt, and then his chest panel; kneeling down, he began inserting his hands into the microtool gloves. Pausing, he looked up at her and said, "I found out I'm an electric ant. Which from one standpoint opens up certain possibilities, which I am exploring now." He flexed his fingers and, at the far end of the left waldo, a micro screwdriver moved, magnified into visibility by the enlarging-lens system. "You can watch," he informed her. "If you so desire."

She had begun to cry.

"What's the matter?" he demanded savagely, without looking up from his work.

"I—it's just so sad. You've been such a good employer to all of us at Tri-Plan. We respect you so. And now it's all changed."

The plastic tape had an unpunched margin at top and bottom; he cut a horizontal strip, very narrow, then, after a moment of great concentration, cut the tape itself four hours away from the scanning head. He then rotated the cut strip into a right-angle piece in relation to the scanner, fused it in place with a micro heat element, then reattached the tape reel to its left and right sides. He had, in effect, inserted a dead twenty minutes into the unfolding flow of his reality. It would take effect—according to his calculations—a few minutes after midnight.

"Are you fixing yourself?" Sarah asked timidly.

Poole said, "I'm freeing myself." Beyond this he had several other alterations in mind. But first he had to test his theory; blank, unpunched tape meant no stimuli, in which case the *lack* of tape . . .

"That look on your face," Sarah said. She began gathering up her purse, coat, rolled-up aud-vid magazine. "I'll go; I can see how you feel about finding me here."

"Stay," he said. "I'll watch the captain kirk with you." He got into his shirt. "Remember years ago when there were— what was it?—twenty or twenty-two TV channels? Before the government shut down the independents?"

She nodded.

"What would it have looked like," he said, "if this TV set projected all channels onto the cathode-ray screen *at the same time*? Could we have distinguished anything, in the mixture?"

"I don't think so."

"Maybe we could learn to. Learn to be selective; do our own job of perceiving what we wanted to and what we didn't. Think of the possibilities, if our brain could handle twenty images at once; think of the amount of knowledge which could be stored during a given period. I wonder if the brain, the human brain—" He broke off. "The human brain couldn't do it," he said, presently, reflecting to himself. "But in theory a quasi-organic brain might."

"Is that what you have?" Sarah asked.

"Yes," Poole said.

They watched the captain kirk to its end, and then they went to bed. But Poole sat up against his pillows smoking and brooding. Beside him, Sarah stirred restlessly, wondering why he did not turn off the light.

Eleven fifty. It would happen any time, now.

"Sarah," he said, "I want your help. In a very few minutes something strange will happen to me. It won't last long, but I want you to watch me carefully. See if I—" He gestured. "Show any changes. If I seem to go to sleep, or if I talk nonsense, or—" He wanted to say, if I disappear. But he did not. "I won't do you any harm, but I think it might be a good idea if you armed yourself. Do you have your anti-mugging gun with you?"

"In my purse." She had become fully awake now; sitting up in bed, she gazed at him with wild fright, her ample shoulders tanned and freckled in the light of the room.

He got her gun for her.

The room stiffened into paralyzed immobility. Then the colors began to drain away. Objects diminished until, smokelike, they flitted away into shadows. Darkness filmed everything as the objects in the room bescame weaker and weaker.

The last stimuli are dying out, Poole realized. He squinted, trying to see. He made out Sarah Benton, sitting in the bed: a two-dimensional figure that, doll-like, had been propped up, there to fade and dwindle. Random gusts of dematerialized substance eddied about in unstable clouds; the elements collected, fell apart, then collected once again. And then the last heat, energy and light dissipated; the room closed over and fell into itself, as if sealed off from reality. And at that point absolute blackness replaced everything, space without depth, not nocturnal but rather stiff and unyielding. And in addition he heard nothing.

Reaching, he tried to touch something. But he had nothing to reach with. Awareness of his own body had departed along with everything else in the universe. He had no hands, and even if he had, there would be nothing for them to feel.

I am still right about the way the damn tape works, he said to himself, using a nonexistent mouth to communicate an invisible message.

Will this pass in ten minutes? he asked himself. Am I right about that, too? He waited . . . but knew intuitively that his time sense had departed with everything else. I can only wait, he realized. And hope it won't be long.

To pace himself, he thought, I'll make up an encyclopedia; I'll try to list everything that begins with an ''a.'' Let's see. He pondered. Apply, automobile, acksetron, atmosphere, Atlantic, tomato aspic, advertising—he thought on and on, categories slithering through his fright-haunted mind.

All at once light flickered on.

He lay on the couch in the living room, and mild sunlight

spilled in through the single window. Two men bent over him, their hands full of tools. Maintenance men, he realized. They've been working on me.

"He's conscious," one of the technicians said. He rose, stood back; Sarah Benton, dithering with anxiety, replaced him.

"Thank god!" she said, breathing wetly in Poole's ear. "I was so afraid; I called Mr. Danceman finally about—"

"What happened?" Poole broke in harshly. "Start from the beginning and for god's sake speak slowly. So I can assimilate it all."

Sarah composed herself, paused to rub her nose, and then plunged on nervously, "You passed out. You just lay there, as if you were dead. I waited until two thirty and you did nothing. I called Mr. Danceman, waking him up, unfortunately, and he called the electric-ant maintenance—I mean, the organic-roby maintenance people, and these two men came about four forty-five, and they've been working on you ever since. It's now six fifteen in the morning. And I'm very cold and I want to go to bed; I can't make it into the office today; I really can't." She turned away, sniffling. The sound annoyed him.

One of the uniformed maintenance men said, "You've been playing around with your reality tape."

"Yes," Poole said. Why deny it? Obviously they had found the inserted solid strip. "I shouldn't have been out that long," he said. "I inserted a ten-minute strip only."

"It shut off the tape transport," the technician explained. "The tape stopped moving forward; your insertion jammed it, and it automatically shut down to avoid tearing the tape. Why would you want to fiddle around with that? Don't you know what you could do?"

"I'm not sure," Poole said.

"But you have a good idea."

Poole said acridly, "That's why I'm doing it."

"Your bill," the maintenance man said, "is going to be ninety-five frogs. Payable in installments, if you so desire."

"Okay," he said; he sat up groggily, rubbed his eyes and grimaced. His head ached and his stomach felt totally empty.

"Shave the tape next time,' the primary technician told him. "That way it won't jam. Didn't it occur to you that it had a safety factor built into it? So it would stop rather than—"

"What happens," Poole interrupted, his voice low and intently careful, "if no tape passes under the scanner? No tape— nothing at all. The photocell shining upward without impedance."

The technicians glanced at each other. One said, "All the neurocircuits jump their gaps and short out."

"Meaning what?" Poole said.

"Meaning it's the end of the mechanism."

Poole said, "I've examined the circuit. It doesn't carry enough voltage to do that. Metal won't fuse under such slight loads of current, even if the terminals are touching. We're talking about a millionth of a watt along a cesium channel perhaps a sixteenth of an inch in length. Let's assume there are a billion possible combinations at one instant arising from the punch-outs on the tape. The total output isn't cumulative; the amount of current depends on what the battery details for that module, and it's not much. With all gates open and going."

"Would we lie?" one of the technicians asked wearily.

"Why not?" Poole said. "Here I have an opportunity to experience everything. Simultaneously. To know the universe in its entirety, to be momentarily in contact with all reality. Something that no human can do. A symphonic score entering my brain outside of time, all notes, all instruments sounding at once. And all symphonies. Do you see?"

"It'll burn you out," both technicians said, together.

"I don't think so," Poole said.

Sarah said, "Would you like a cup of coffee, Mr. Poole?"

"Yes," he said; he lowered his legs, pressed his cold feet against the floor, shuddered. He then stood up. His body ached. They had me lying all night on the couch, he realized. All things considered, they could have done better than that.

At the kitchen table in the far corner of the room, Garson Poole sat sipping coffee across from Sarah. The technicians had long since gone.

"You're not going to try any more experiments on yourself, are you?" Sarah asked wistfully.

Poole grated, "I would like to control time. To reverse it." I will cut a segment of tape out, he thought, and fuse it in upside down. The causal sequences will then flow the other way. Thereupon I will walk backward down the steps from the roof field, back up to my door, push a locked door open, walk backward to the sink, where I will get out a stack of dirty dishes. I will seat myself at this table before the stack, fill each dish with food produced from my stomach. . . . I will then transfer the food to the refrigerator, pack it in bags, carry the bags to a supermarket, distribute the food here and there in the store. And at last, at the front counter, they will pay me money for this, from their cash register. The food will be packed with other food in big plastic boxes, shipped out of the city into the hydroponic plants on the Atlantic, there to be joined back to trees and bushes or the bodies of dead animals or pushed deep into the ground. But what would all this prove? A video tape running backward. . . . I would know no more than I know now, which is not enough.

What I want, he realized, is ultimate and absolute reality, for one microsecond. After that it doesn't matter, because all will be known; nothing will be left to understand or see.

I might try one other change, he said to himself. Before I try cutting the tape. I will prick new punch-holes in the tape and see what presently emerges. It will be interesting because I will not know what the holes I make mean.

Using the tip of a microtool, he punched several holes, at random, on the tape. As close to the scanner as he could manage . . . he did not want to wait.

"I wonder if you'll see it," he said to Sarah. Apparently not, insofar as he could extrapolate. "Something may show up," he said to her. "I just want to warn you; I don't want you to be afraid."

"Oh, dear," Sarah said tinnily.

He examined his wristwatch. One minute passed, then a second, a third. And then—

In the center of the room appeared a flock of green and black ducks. They quacked excitedly, rose from the floor, fluttered against the ceiling in a dithering mass of feathers and wings in the vast urge, their instinct to get away.

"Ducks," Poole said, marveling. "I punched a hole for a flight of wild ducks."

Now something else appeared. A park bench with an elderly, tattered man seated on it, reading a torn, bent newspaper. He looked up, dimly made out Poole, smiled briefly at him with badly made dentures, and then returned to his folded-back newspaper. He read on.

"Do you see him?" Poole asked Sarah. "And the ducks." At that moment the ducks and the park bum disappeared. Nothing remained of them. The interval of their punch-holes had quickly passed.

"They weren't real," Sarah said. "Were they? So how—"

"You're not real," he told Sarah. "You're a stimulus-factor on my reality tape. A punch-hole that can be glazed over. Do you also have an existence in another reality tape, or one in an objective reality?" He did not know; he couldn't tell. Perhaps she existed in a thousand reality tapes; perhaps on every reality tape ever manufactured. "If I cut the tape," he said, "you will be everywhere and nowhere. Like everything else in the universe. At least as far as I'm aware of it."

Sarah faltered. "I'm real."

"I want to know you completely," Poole said. "To do that I must cut the tape. If I don't do it now, I'll do it some other time; it's inevitable that eventually I'll do it." So why wait? he asked himself. And there is always the possibility that Danceman has reported back to my maker, that they will be making moves to head me off. Because, perhaps, I'm endangering their property—myself.

"You make me wish I had gone to the office after all," Sarah said, her mouth turned down with dimpled gloom.

"Go," Poole said.

"I don't want to leave you alone."

"I'll be fine," Poole said.

"No, you're not going to be fine. You're going to unplug yourself or something, kill yourself because you've found out you're just an electric ant and not a human being."

He said, presently, "Maybe so." Maybe it boiled down to that.

"And I can't stop you," she said.

"No." He nodded in agreement. "But I'm going to stay," Sarah said. "Even if I can't stop you. Because if I do leave and you do kill yourself, I'll always ask myself for the rest of my life what would have happened if I had stayed. You see?"

Again he nodded.

"Go ahead," Sarah said.

He rose to his feet. "It's not pain I'm going to feel," he told her. "Although it may look like that to you. Keep in mind the fact that organic robots have minimal pain-circuits in them. I will be experiencing the most intense—"

"Don't tell me any more," she broke in. "Just do it if you're going to, or don't do it if you're not."

Clumsily—because he was frightened—he wriggled his hands into the microglove assembly, reached to pick up a tiny tool: a sharp cutting blade. "I am going to cut a tape mounted inside my chest panel," he said, as he gazed through the enlarging-lens system. "That's all." His hand shook as it lifted the cutting blade. In a second it can be done, he realized. All over. And—I will have time to fuse the cut ends of tape back together, he realized. A half-hour at least. If I change my mind.

He cut the tape.

Staring at him, cowering, Sarah whispered, "Nothing happened."

"I have thirty or forty minutes." He reseated himself at the table, having drawn his hands from the gloves. His voice, he noticed, shook; undoubtedly Sarah was aware of it, and he felt anger at himself, knowing that he had alarmed her. "I'm sorry," he said, irrationally; he wanted to apologize to her. "Maybe you ought to leave," he said in panic; again he stood up. So did she, reflexively, as if imitating him; bloated and nervous, she stood there palpitating. "Go away," he said thickly. "Back to the office, where you ought to be. Where we both ought to be." I'm going to fuse the tape-ends together, he told himself; the tension is too great for me to stand.

Reaching his hands toward the gloves he groped to pull them over his straining fingers. Peering into the enlarging screen, he saw the beam from the photoelectric gleam upward, pointed directly into the scanner; at the same time he saw the end of the tape disappearing under the scanner . . . he saw this, understood it; I'm too late, he realized. It has passed through. God, he thought, help me. It has begun winding at a rate greater than I calculated. So it's *now* that—

He saw apples and cobblestones and zebras. He felt warmth,

the silky texture of cloth; he felt the ocean lapping at him and a great wind, from the north, plucking at him as if to lead him somewhere. Sarah was all around him, so was Danceman. New York glowed in the night, and the squibs about him scuttled and bounced through night skies and daytime and flooding and drought. Butter relaxed into liquid on his tongue, and at the same time hideous odors and tastes assailed him: the bitter presence of poisons and lemons and blades of summer grass. He drowned; he fell; he lay in the arms of a woman in a vast white bed which at the same time dinned shrilly in his ear: the warning noise of a defective elevator in one of the ancient, ruined downtown hotels. I am living, I have lived, I will never live, he said to himself, and with his thoughts came every word, every sound; insects squeaked and raced, and he half sank into a complex body of homeostatic machinery located somewhere in Tri-Plan's labs.

He wanted to say something to Sarah. Opening his mouth, he tried to bring forth words—a specific string of them out of the enormous mass of them brilliantly lighting his mind, scorching him with their utter meaning.

His mouth burned. He wondered why.

Frozen against the wall, Sarah Benton opened her eyes and saw the curl of smoke ascending from Poole's half-opened mouth. Then the roby sank down, knelt on elbows and knees, then slowly spread out in a broken, crumpled heap. She knew without examining it that it had "died."

Poole did it to itself, she realized. And it couldn't feel pain; it said so itself. Or at least not very much pain; maybe a little. Anyway, now it is over.

I had better call Mr. Danceman and tell him what's happened, she decided. Still shaky, she made her way across the room to the fone; picking it up, she dialed from memory.

It thought I was a stimulus-factor on its reality tape, she said to herself. So it thought I would die when it "died." How strange, she thought. Why did it imagine that? It had never been plugged into the real world; it had "lived" in an electronic world of its own. How bizarre.

"Mr. Danceman," she said, when the circuit to his office had been put through. "Poole is gone. It destroyed itself right in front of my eyes. You'd better come over."

"So we're finally free of it."

"Yes, won't it be nice?"

Danceman said, "I'll send a couple of men over from the shop." He saw past her, made out the sight of Poole lying by the kitchen table. "You go home and rest," he instructed Sarah. "You must be worn out by all this."

"Yes," she said. "Thank you, Mr. Danceman." She hung up and stood, aimlessly.

And then she noticed something.

My hands, she thought. She held them up. Why is it I can see through them?

The wall of the room, too, had become ill-defined.

Trembling, she walked back to the inert roby, stood by it, not knowing what to do. Through her legs the carpet showed, and then the carpet became dim, and she saw, through it, further layers of disintegrating matter beyond.

Maybe if I can fuse the tape-ends together, she thought. But she did not know how. And already Poole had become vague.

The wind of early morning blew about her. She did not feel it; she had begun, now, to cease to feel.

The winds blew on.

THE GOLEM
Avram Davidson

The Golem is an android-figure out of old Jewish fable—miraculously brought back to life in this charming and playful short story by a master of comic fantasy.

The gray-faced person came along the street where old Mr. and Mrs. Gumbeiner lived. It was afternoon, it was autumn, the sun was warm and soothing to their ancient bones. Anyone who attended the movies in the twenties or the early thirties has seen that street a thousand times. Past these bungalows with their half-double roofs Edmund Lowe walked arm-in-arm with Leatrice Joy and Harold Lloyd was chased by Chinamen waving hatchets. Under these squamous palm trees Laurel kicked Hardy and Woolsey beat Wheeler upon the head with a codfish. Across these pocket-handkerchief-sized lawns the juveniles of Our Gang comedies pursued one another and were pursued by angry fat men in golf knickers. On this same street—or perhaps on some other one of five hundred streets exactly like it.

Mrs. Gumbeiner indicated the gray-faced person to her husband.

"You think maybe he's got something the matter?" she asked. "He walks kind of funny, to me."

"Walks like a *golem*," Mr. Gumbeiner said indifferently.

The old woman was nettled.

"Oh, I don't know," she said. "*I* think he walks like your cousin Mendel."

The old man pursed his mouth angrily and chewed on his pipestem. The gray-faced person turned up the concrete path, walked up the steps to the porch, sat down in a chair. Old Mr. Gumbeiner ignored him. His wife stared at the stranger.

"Man comes in without a hello, goodby, or how-are-you, sits himself down and right away he's at home . . . The chair is comfortable?" she asked. "Would you like a glass tea?"

She turned to her husband.

"Say something, Gumbeiner!" she demanded. "What are you, made of wood?"

The old man smiled a slow, wicked, triumphant smile.

"Why should *I* say anything?" he asked the air. "Who am I? Nothing, that's who."

The stranger spoke. His voice was harsh and monotonous.

"When you learn who—or, rather, what—I am, the flesh will melt from your bones in terror." He bared porcelain teeth.

"Never mind about my bones!" the old woman cried. "You've got a lot of nerve talking about my bones!"

"You will quake with fear," said the stranger. Old Mrs. Gumbeiner said that she hoped he would live so long. She turned to her husband once again.

"Gumbeiner, when are you going to mow the lawn?"

"All mankind—" the stranger began.

"*Shah*! I'm talking to my husband. . . . He talks *eppis* kind of funny, Gumbeiner, no?"

"Probably a foreigner," Mr. Gumbeiner said, complacently.

"You think so?" Mrs. Gumbeiner glanced fleetingly at the stranger. "He's got a very bad color in his face, *nebbich*, I suppose he came to California for his health."

" Disease, pain, sorrow, love, grief—all are nought to—"
Mr. Gumbeiner cut in on the stranger's statement.

"Gall bladder," the old man said. "Guinzburg down at the
shule looked exactly the same before his operation. Two profes-
sors they had in for him, and a private nurse day and night."

"I am not a human being!" the stranger said loudly.

"Three thousand seven hundred fifty dollars it cost his son,
Guinzburg told me. 'For you, Poppa, nothing is too expen-
sive—only get well,' the son told him."

"*I am not a human being!*"

"Ai, is that a son for you!" the old woman said, rocking
her head. "A heart of gold, pure gold." She looked at the
stranger. "All right, all right, I heard you the first time. Gumbeiner! I asked you a question. When are you going to cut the
lawn?"

"On Wednesday, *odder* maybe Thursday, comes the Japaneser to the neighborhood. To cut lawns is *his* profession. *My*
profession is to be a glazier—retired."

"Between me and all mankind is an inevitable hatred," the
stranger said. "When I tell you what I am, the flesh will
melt—"

"You said, you said already," Mr. Gumbeiner interrupted.

"In Chicago where the winters were as cold and bitter as the
Czar of Russia's heart," the old woman intoned, "you had the
strength to carry the frames with the glass together day in and
day out. But in California with the golden sun to mow the lawn
when your wife asks, for this you have no strength. Do I call in
the Japaneser to cook for you supper?"

"Thirty years Professor Allardyce spent perfecting his
theories. Electronics, neuronics—"

"Listen, how educated he talks," Mr. Gumbeiner said, admiringly. "Maybe he goes to the University here?"

"If he goes to the University, maybe he knows Bud?" his
wife suggested.

"Probably they're in the same class and he came to see him about the homework, no?"

"Certainly he must be in the same class. How many classses are there? Five *in ganzen*: Bud showed me on his program card." She counted off on her fingers. "Television Appreciation and Criticism, Small Boat Building, Social Adjustment, The American Dance.... The American Dance—*nu*, Gumbeiner—"

"Contemporary Ceramics," her husband said, relishing the syllables. "A fine boy, Bud. A pleasure to have him for a boarder."

"After thirty years spent in these studies," the stranger, who had continued to speak unnoticed, went on, "he turned from the theoretical to the pragmatic. In ten years' time he had made the most titanic discovery in history: he made mankind, *all* mankind, superfluous; he made *me*."

"What did Tillie write in her last letter?" asked the old man.

The old woman shrugged.

"What should she write? The same thing. Sidney was home from the Army, Naomi has a new boyfriend—"

"*He made ME!*"

"Listen, Mr. Whatever-your-name-is," the old woman said, "maybe where you come from is different, but in *this* country you don't interrupt people the while they're talking.... Hey. Listen—what do you mean, he *made* you? What kind of talk is that?"

The stranger bared all his teeth again, exposing the too-pink gums.

"In his library, to which I had a more complete access after his sudden and as yet undiscovered death from entirely natural causes, I found a complete collection of stories about androids, from Shelley's *Frankenstein* through Čapek's *R.U.R.* to Asimov's—"

"Frankenstein?" said the old man, with interest. "There

used to be a Frankenstein who had the soda-*wasser* place on Halstead Street—a Litvack, *nebbich.*''

''What are you talking?'' Mrs. Gumbeiner demanded. ''His name was Franken*thal*, and it wasn't on Halstead, it was on Roosevelt.''

''—clearly shown that all mankind has an instinctive antipathy towards androids and there will always be an inevitable struggle between them—''

''Of course, of course!'' Old Mr. Gumbeiner clicked his teeth against his pipe. ''I am always wrong, you are always right. How could you stand to be married to such a stupid person all this time?''

''I don't know,'' the old woman said. ''Sometimes I wonder, myself. I think it must be his good looks.'' She began to laugh. Old Mr. Gumbeiner blinked, then began to smile, then took his wife's hand.

''Foolish old woman,'' the stranger said. ''Why do you laugh? Do you not know I have come to destroy you?''

''What?'' old Mr. Gumbeiner shouted. ''Close your mouth, you!'' He darted from the chair and struck the stranger with the flat of his hand. The stranger's head struck against the porch pillar and bounced back.

''When you talk to my wife, talk respectable, you hear?''

Old Mrs. Gumbeiner, cheeks very pink, pushed her husband back to his chair. Then she leaned forward and examined the stranger's head. She clicked her tongue as she pulled aside a flap of gray, skinlike material.

''Gumbeiner, look! He's all springs and wires inside!''

''I *told* you he was a *golem*, but no, you wouldn't listen,'' the old man said.

''You said he *walked* like a *golem*.''

''How could he walk like a *golem* unless he *was* one?''

''All right, all right. . . . You broke him, so now fix him.''

"My grandfather, his light shines from Paradise, told me that when MoHaRaL—Morenyu Ha-Rav Löw—his memory for a blessing, made the *golem* in Prague, three hundred? four hundred years ago? he wrote on his forehead the Holy Name."

Smiling reminiscently, the old woman continued. "And the *golem* cut the rabbi's wood and brought his water and guarded the ghetto."

"And one time only he disobeyed the Rabbi Löw, and Rabbi Löw erased the *Shem Ha-Mephorash* from the *golem*'s forehead and the *golem* fell down like a dead one. And they put him up in the attic of the *shule* and he's still there today if the Communisten haven't sent him to Moscow. . . .This is not just a story," he said.

"*Avadda* not!" said the old woman.

"I myself have seen both the *shule and* the rabbi's grave," her husband said, conclusively.

"But I think this must be a different kind of *golem*, Gumbeiner. See, on his forehead; nothing written."

"What's the matter, there's a law I can't write something there? Where is that lump clay Bud brought us from his class?"

The old man washed his hands, adjusted his little black skullcap, and slowly and carefully wrote four Hebrew letters on the gray forehead.

"Ezra the Scribe himself couldn't do better," the old woman said, admiringly. "Nothing happens," she observed, looking at the lifeless figure sprawled in the chair.

"Well, after all, am I Rabbi Löw?" her husband asked, deprecatingly. "No," he answered. He leaned over and examined the exposed mechanism. "This spring goes here . . . this wire comes with this one. . . ." The figure moved. "But this one goes where? And this one?"

"Let be," said his wife. The figure sat up slowly and rolled its eyes loosely.

"Listen, Reb *Golem*," the old man said, wagging his finger. "Pay attention to what I say—you understand?"

"Understand. . . ."

"If you want to stay here, you got to do like Mr. Gumbeiner says."

"Do-like-Mr.-Gumbeiner-says. . . ."

"*That's* the way I like to hear a *golem* talk. Malka, give here the mirror from the pocketbook. Look, you see your face? You see on the forehead, what's written? If you don't do like Mr. Gumbeiner says, he'll wipe out what's written and you'll be no more alive."

"No-more-alive. . . ."

"*That's* right. Now, listen. Under the porch you'll find a lawnmower. Take it. And cut the lawn. Then come back. Go."

"Go. . . ." The figure shambled down the stairs. Presently the sound of the lawnmower whirred through the quiet air in the street just like the street where Jackie Cooper shed huge tears on Wallace Beery's shirt and Chester Conklin rolled his eyes at Marie Dressler.

"So what will you write to Tillie?" old Mr. Gumbeiner asked.

"What should I write?" old Mrs. Gumbeiner shrugged. "I'll write that the weather is lovely out here and that we are both, Blessed be the Name, in good health."

The old man nodded his head slowly, and they sat together on the front porch in the warm afternoon sun.

FONDLY FAHRENHEIT

Alfred Bester

And finally, a splendid display of fireworks—Alfred Bester's classic story of murder and nightmarish identity-shifts, of rising temperature and crumbling sanity. Who is master, who is slave, asks Bester—and the author of The Demolished Man and The Stars My Destination supplies a brilliant, unforgettable answer.

He doesn't know which of us we are these days, but they know one truth. You must own nothing but yourself. You must make your own life, live your own life and die your own death . . . or else you will die another's.

The rice fields on Paragon III stretch for hundreds of miles like checkerboard tundras, a blue and brown mosaic under a burning sky of orange. In the evening, clouds whip like smoke, and the paddies rustle and murmur.

A long line of men marched across the paddies the evening we escaped from Paragon III. They were silent, armed, intent; a long rank of silhouetted statues looming against the smoking sky. Each man carried a gun. Each man wore a walkie-talkie belt pack, the speaker button in his ear, the microphone bug clipped to his throat, the glowing view-screen strapped to his wrist like a green-eyed watch. The multitude of screens showed nothing but a multitude of individual paths through the paddies. the annunciators made no sound but the rustle and splash of steps. The men spoke infrequently, in heavy grunts, all speaking to all.

"Nothing here."

"Where's here?"

"Jenson's fields."

"You're drifting too far west."

"Close in the line there."

"Anybody covered the Grimson paddy?"

"Yeah. Nothing."

"She couldn't have walked this far."

"Could have been carried."

"Think she's alive?"

"Why should she be dead?"

The slow refrain swept up and down the long line of beaters advancing toward the smoky sunset. The line of beaters wavered like a writhing snake, but never ceased its remorseless advance. One hundred men spaced fifty feet apart. Five thousand feet of ominous search. One mile of angry determination stretching from east to west across a compass of heart. Evening fell. Each man lit his search lamp. The writhing snake was transformed into a necklace of wavering diamonds.

"Clear here. Nothing."

"Nothing here."

"Nothing."

"What about the Allen paddies?"

"Covering them now."

"Think we missed her?"

"Maybe."

"We'll beat back and check."

"This'll be an all-night job."

"Allen paddies clear."

"God damn! We've got to find her!"

"We'll find her."

"Here she is. Sector Seven. Tune in."

The line stopped. The diamonds froze in the heat. There was silence. Each man gazed into the glowing green screen on his wrist, tuning to Sector 7. All tuned to one. All showed a small nude figure awash in the muddy water of a paddy. Alongside the figure an owner's stake of bronze read: VANDALEUR. The ends of the line converged toward the Vandaleur field. The necklace turned into a cluster of stars. One hundred men gathered around a small nude body, a child dead in a rice paddy. There was no water in her mouth. There were finger-marks on her throat. Her innocent face was battered. Her body was torn. Clotted blood on her skin was crusted and hard.

"Dead three–four hours at least."

"Her mouth is dry."

"She wasn't drowned. Beaten to death."

In the dark evening heat the men swore softly. They picked up the body. One stopped the others and pointed to the child's fingernails. She had fought her murderer. Under the nails were particles of flesh and bright drops of scarlet red, still liquid, still uncoagulated.

"That blood ought to be clotted too."

"Funny."

"Not so funny. What kind of blood don't clot?'

"Android."

"Looks like she was killed by one."

"Vandaleur owns an android."

"She couldn't be killed by an android."

"That's android blood under her nails."

"The police better check."

"The police'll prove I'm right."

"But androids can't kill."

"That's android blood, ain't it?"

"Androids can't kill. They're made that way."

"Looks like one android was made wrong."

"Jesus!"

And the thermometer that day registered 92.9° gloriously Fahrenheit.

So there we were aboard the *Paragon Queen* en route for Megastar V, James Vandaleur and his android. James Vandaleur counted his money and wept. In the second-class cabin with him was his android, a magnificent synthetic creature with classic features and wide blue eyes. Raised on its forehead in a cameo of flesh were the letters MA, indicating that this was one of the rare multiple-aptitude androids, worth $57,000 on the current exchange. There we were, weeping and counting and calmly watching.

"Twelve, fourteen, sixteen. Sixteen hundred dollars." Vandaleur wept. "That's all. Sixteen hundred dollars. My house was worth ten thousand. The land was worth five. There was furniture, cars, my paintings, etchings, my plane, my— And nothing to show for everything but sixteen hundred dollars."

I leaped up from the table and turned on the android. I pulled a strap from one of the leather bags and beat the android. It didn't move.

"I must remind you," the android said, "that I am worth fifty-seven thousand dollars on the current exchange. I must warn you that you are endangering valuable property."

"You damned crazy machine," Vandaleur shouted.

"I am not a machine," the android answered. "The robot is a machine. The android is a chemical creation of synthetic tissue."

"What got into you?" Vandaleur cried. "Why did you do it? Damn you!" He beat the android savagely.

"I must remind you that I cannot be punished," it said. "The pleasure-pain syndrome is not incorporated in the android synthesis."

"Then why did you kill her?" Vandaleur shouted. "If it wasn't for kicks, why did you—"

"I must remind you," the android said, "that the second-class cabins in these ships are not soundproofed."

Vandaleur dropped the strap and stood panting, staring at the creature he owned.

"Why did you do it? Why did you kill her?" I asked.

"I don't know," I answered.

"First it was malicious mischief. Small things. Petty destruction. I should have known there was something wrong with you then. Androids can't destroy. They can't harm. They—"

"There is no pleasure-pain syndrome incorporated in the android synthesis."

"Then it got to arson. Then serious destruction. Then assault . . . that engineer on Rigel. Each time worse. Each time we had to get out faster. Now it's murder. Christ! What's the matter with you? What's happened?"

"There are no self-check relays incorporated in the android brain."

"Each time we had to get out it was a step downhill. Look at me. In a second-class cabin. Me. James Paleologue Vandaleur. There was a time when my father was the wealthiest— Now, sixteen hundred dollars in the world. That's all I've got. And you. Christ damn you!"

Vandaleur raised the strap to beat the android again, then dropped it and collapsed on a berth, sobbing. At last he pulled himself together.

"Instructions," he said.

The multiple-aptitude android responded at once. It arose and awaited orders.

"My name is now Valentine. James Valentine. I stopped off on Paragon Three for only one day to transfer to this ship for Megastar five. My occupation: Agent for one privately owned MA android which is for hire. Purpose of visit: To settle on Megastar Five. Forge the papers."

The android removed Vandaleur's passport and papers from a bag, got pen and ink and sat down at the table. With an accurate, flawless hand—an accomplished hand that could draw, write, paint, carve, engrave, etch, photograph, design, create and build—it meticulously forged new credentials for Vandaleur. Its owner watched me miserable.

"Create and build," I muttered. "And now destroy. Oh, God! What am I going to do? Christ! If I could only get rid of you. If I didn't have to live off you. God! If only I'd inherited some guts instead of you."

Dallas Brady was Megastar's leading jewelry designer. She was short, stocky, amoral and a nymphomaniac. She hired Valentine's multiple-aptitude android and put me to work in her shop. She seduced Valentine. In her bed one night, she asked abruptly: "Your name's Vandaleur, isn't it?"

"Yes," I murmured. Then: "No! No! It's Valentine. James Valentine."

"What happened on Paragon?" Dallas Brady asked. "I thought androids couldn't kill or destroy property. Prime Directives and Inhibitions set up for them when they're synthesized. Every company guarantees they can't."

"Valentine!" Vandaleur insisted.

"Oh, come off it," Dallas Brady said. "I've known for a week. I haven't hollered copper, have I?"

"The name is Valentine."

"You want to prove it? You want I should call the police?" Dallas reached out and picked up the phone.

"For God's sake, Dallas!" Vandaleur leaped up and struggled to take the phone from her. She fended him off, laughing at him, until he collapsed and wept in shame and helplessness.

"How did you find out?" he asked at last.

"The papers are full of it. And Valentine was a little too close to Vandaleur. That wasn't smart, was it?"

"I guess not. I'm not very smart."

"Your android's got quite a record, hasn't it? Assault. Arson. Destruction. What happened on Paragon?"

"It kidnapped a child. Took her out into the rice fields and murdered her."

"Raped her?"

"I don't know."

"They're going to catch up with you."

"Don't I know it? Christ! We've been running for two years now. Seven planets in two years. I must have abandoned a hundred thousand dollars' worth of property in two years."

"You better find out what's wrong with it."

"How can I? Can I walk into a repair clinic and ask for an overhaul? What am I going to say? 'My android's just turned killer. Fix it.' They'd call the police right off." I began to shake. "They'd have that android dismantled inside one day. I'd probably be booked as an accessory to murder."

"Why didn't you have it repaired before it got to murder?"

"I couldn't take the chance," Vandaleur explained angrily. "If they started fooling around with lobotomies and body chemistry and endocrine surgery, they might have destroyed its aptitudes. What would I have left to hire out? How would I live?"

"You could work yourself. People do."

"Work at what? You know I'm good for nothing. How could I compete with specialist androids and robots? Who can, unless he's got a terrific talent for a particular job?"

"Yeah. That's true."

"I lived off my old man all my life. Damn him! He had to go bust just before he died. Left me the android and that's all. The only way I can get along is living off what it earns."

"You better sell it before the cops catch up with you. You can live off fifty grand. Invest it."

"At three percent? Fifteen hundred a year? When the android returns fifteen percent of its value? Eight thousand a year. That's what it earns. No, Dallas. I've got to go along with it."

"What are you going to do about its violence kick?"

"I can't do anything . . . except watch it and pray. What are you going to do about it?"

"Nothing. It's none of my business. Only one thing . . . I ought to get something for keeping my mouth shut."

"What?"

"The android works for me for free. Let somebody else pay you, but I get it for free."

The multiple-aptitude android worked. Vandaleur collected its fees. His expenses were taken care of. His savings began to mount. As the warm spring of Megastar V turned to hot summer, I began investigating farms and properties. It would be possible, within a year or two, for us to settle down permanently, provided Dallas Brady's demands did not become rapacious.

On the first hot day of summer, the android began singing in Dallas Brady's workshop. It hovered over the electric furnace which, along with the weather, was broiling the shop, and sang an ancient tune that had been popular half a century before.

> Oh, it's no feat to beat the heat.
> All reet! All reet!
> So jeet your seat

Be fleet be fleet
Cool and discreet
Honey . . .

It sang in a strange, halting voice, and its accomplished fingers were clasped behind its back, writhing in a strange rumba all their own. Dallas Brady was surprised.

"You happy or something?" she asked.

"I must remind you that the pleasure-pain syndrome is not incorporated in the android synthesis," I answered. "All reet! All reet! Be fleet be fleet, cool and discreet, honey . . . "

Its fingers stopped their twisting and picked up a pair of iron tongs. The android poked them into the glowing heart of the furnace, leaning far forward to peer into the lovely heat.

"Be careful, you damned fool!" Dallas Brady exclaimed. "You want to fall in?"

"I must remind you that I am worth fifty-seven thousand dollars on the current exchange," I said. "It is forbidden to endanger valuable property. All reet! All reet! Honey . . ."

It withdrew a crucible of glowing gold from the electric furnace, turned, capered hideously, sang crazily, and splashed a sluggish gobbet of molten gold over Dallas Brady's head. She screamed and collapsed, her hair and clothes flaming, her skin crackling. The android poured again while it capered and sang.

"Be fleet be fleet, cool and discreet, honey . . ." It sang and slowly poured and poured the molten gold until the writhing body was still. Then I left the workshop and rejoined James Vandaleur in his hotel suite. The android's charred clothes and squirming fingers warned its owner that something was very much wrong.

Vandaleur rushed to Dallas Brady's workshop, stared once, vomited and fled. I had enough time to pack one bag and raise nine hundred dollars on portable assets. He took a third-class cabin on the *Megastar Queen*, which left that morning for Lyre Alpha. He took me with him. He wept and counted his money and I beat the android again.

And the thermometer in Dallas Brady's workshop registered 98.1° beautifully Fahrenheit.

On Lyra Alpha we holed up in a small hotel near the university. There, Vandaleur carefully bruised my forehead until the letters MA were obliterated by the swelling and the discoloration. The letters would reappear again, but not for several months, and in the meantime Vandaleur hoped that the hue and cry for an MA android would be forgotten. The android was hired out as a common laborer in the university power plant. Vandaleur, as James Venice, eked out life on the android's small earnings.

I wasn't too unhappy. Most of the other residents in the hotel were university students, equally hard up, but delightfully young and enthusiastic. There was one charming girl with sharp eyes and a quick mind. Her name was Wanda, and she and her beau, Jed Stark, took a tremendous interest in the killing android which was being mentioned in every paper in the galaxy.

"We've been studying the case," she and Jed said at one of the casual student parties which happened to be held this night in Vandaleur's room. "We think we know what's causing it. We're going to do a paper." They were in a high state of excitement.

"Causing what?" somebody wanted to know.

"The android rampage."

"Obviously out of adjustment, isn't it? Body chemistry gone haywire. Maybe a kind of synthetic cancer, yes?"

"No." Wanda gave Jed a look of suppressed triumph.

"Well, what is it?"

"Something specific."

"What?"

"That would be telling."

"Oh, come on."

"Nothing doing."

"Won't you tell us?" I asked intently. "I . . . We're very much interested in what could go wrong with an android."

"No, Mr. Venice," Wanda said. "It's a unique idea and we've got to protect it. One thesis like this and we'll be set up for life. We can't take the chance of somebody stealing it."

"Can't you give us a hint?"

"No. Not a hint. Don't say a word, Jed. But I'll tell you this much, Mr. Venice. I'd hate to be the man who owns that android."

"You mean the police?" I asked.

"I mean projection, Mr. Venice. Psychotic projection! That's the danger . . . and I won't say any more. I've said too much as is."

I heard steps outside, and a hoarse voice singing softly: "Be fleet be fleet, cool and discreet, honey . . ." My android entered the room, home from its tour of duty at the university power plant. It was not introduced. I motioned to it and I immediately responded to the command and went to the beer keg and took over Vandaleur's job of serving the guests. Its accomplished fingers writhed in a private rumba of their own. Gradually they stopped their squirming, and the strange humming ended.

Androids were not unusual at the university. The wealthier students owned them along with cars and planes. Vandaleur's android provoked no comment, but young Wanda was sharp-eyed and quick-witted. She noted my bruised forehead and she was intent on the history-making thesis she and Jed Stark were going to write. After the party broke up, she consulted with Jed walking upstairs to her room.

"Jed, why'd that android have a bruised forehead?"

"Probably hurt itself, Wanda. It's working in the power plant. They fling a lot of heavy stuff around."

"That all?"

"What else?"

"It could be a convenient bruise."

"Convenient for what?"

"Hiding what's stamped on its forehead."

"No point to that, Wanda. You don't have to see marks on a forehead to recognize an android. You don't have to see a trademark on a car to know it's a car."

"I don't mean it's trying to pass as a human. I mean it's trying to pass as a lower-grade android."

"Why?"

"Suppose it had MA on its forehead."

"Multiple aptitude? Then why in hell would Venice waste it stoking furnaces if it could earn more— Oh. Oh! You mean it's—?"

Wanda nodded.

"Jesus!" Stark pursed his lips. "What do we do? Call the police?"

"No. We don't know if it's an MA for a fact. If it turns out to be an MA and the killing android, our paper comes first anyway. This is our big chance, Jed. If it's *that* android we can run a series of controlled tests and—"

"How do we find out for sure?"

"Easy. Infrared film. That'll show what's under the bruise. Borrow a camera. We'll sneak down to the power plant tomorrow afternoon and take some pictures. Then we'll know."

They stole down into the university power plant the following afternoon. It was a vast cellar, deep under the earth. It was dark, shadowy, luminous with burning light from the furnace doors. Above the roar of the fires they could hear a strange voice shouting and chanting in the echoing vault: "All reet! All reet!

So jeet your seat. Be fleet be fleet, cool and discreet, honey . . ."
And they could see a capering figure dancing a lunatic rumba in
time to the music it shouted. The legs twisted. The arms waved.
The fingers writhed.

Jed Stark raised the camera and began shooting his spool of
infrared film, aiming the camera sights at that bobbing head.
Then Wanda shrieked, for I saw them and came charging down
on them, brandishing a polished steel shovel. It smashed the
camera. It felled the girl and then the boy. Jed fought me for a
desperate hissing moment before he was bludgeoned into helplessness. Then the android dragged them to the furnace and fed
them to the flames, slowly, hideously. It capered and sang.
Then it returned to my hotel.

The thermometer in the power plant registered 100.9° mur-
derously Fahrenheit. All reet! All reet!

We bought steerage on the *Lyra Queen* and Vandaleur and the
android did odd jobs for their meals. During the night watches,
Vandaleur would sit alone in the steerage head with a cardboard
portfolio on his lap, puzzling over its contents. That portfolio
was all he had managed to bring with him from Lyra Alpha. He
had stolen it from Wanda's room. It was labeled ANDROID. It
contained the secret of my sickness.

And it contained nothing but newspapers. Scores of newspa-
pers from all over the galaxy, printed, microfilmed, engraved,
etched, offset, photostated . . . Rigel *Star-Banner* . . . Paragon
Picayune . . . Megastar *Times-Leader* . . . Lalande *Herald* . . .
Lacaille *Journal* . . . Indi *Intelligencer* . . . Eridani *Telegram-
News*. All reet! All reet!

Nothing but newspapers. Each paper contained an account of
one crime in the android's ghastly career. Each paper also
contained news, domestic and foreign, sports, society, weather,
shipping news, stock exchange quotations, human-interest

stories, features, contests, puzzles. Somewhere in that mass of uncollated facts was the secret Wanda and Jed Stark had discovered. Vandaleur pored over the papers helplessly. It was beyond him. So jeet your seat!

"I'll sell you," I told the android. "Damn you. When we land on Terra, I'll sell you. I'll settle for three percent of whatever you're worth."

"I am worth fifty-seven thousand dollars on the current exchange," I told him.

"If I can't sell you, I'll turn you in to the police," I said.

"I am valuable property," I answered. "It is forbidden to endanger valuable property. You won't have me destroyed."

"Christ damn you!" Vandaleur cried. "What? Are you arrogant? Do you know you can trust me to protect you? Is that the secret?"

The multiple-aptitude android regarded him with calm accomplished eyes. "Sometimes," it said, "it is a good thing to be property."

It was three below zero when the *Lyra Queen* dropped at Croydon Field. A mixture of ice and snow swept across the field, fizzling and exploding into steam under the *Queen*'s tail jets. The passengers trotted numbly across the blackened concrete to customs inspection, and thence to the airport bus that was to take them to London. Vandaleur and the android were broke. They walked.

By midnight they reached Piccadilly Circus. The December ice storm had not slackened and the statue of Eros was encrusted with ice. They turned right, walked down to Trafalgar Square and then along the Strand, shaking with cold and wet. Just above Fleet Street, Vandaleur saw a solitary figure coming from the direction of St. Paul's. He drew the android into an alley.

"We've got to have money," he whispered. He pointed to

the approaching figure. "He has money. Take it from him."

"The order cannot be obeyed," the android said.

"Take it from him," Vandaleur repeated. "By force. Do you understand? We're desperate."

"It is contrary to my prime directive," the android repeated. "The order cannot be obeyed."

"Damn you!" I said. "You've murdered . . . tortured . . . destroyed! You tell me that *now*?"

"It is forbidden to endanger life or property. The order cannot be obeyed."

I thrust the android back and leaped out at the stranger. He was tall, austere, poised. He had an air of hope curdled by cynicism. He carried a cane. I saw he was blind.

"Yes?" he said. "I hear you near me. What is it?"

"Sir . . ." Vandaleur hesitated. "I'm desperate."

"We are all desperate," the stranger replied. "Quietly desperate."

"Sir . . . I've got to have some money."

"Are you begging or stealing?" The sightless eyes passed over Vandaleur and the android.

"I'm prepared for either."

"Ah. So are we all. It is the history of our race." The stranger motioned over his shoulder. "I have been begging at St. Paul's, my friend. What I desire cannot be stolen. What is it you desire that you are lucky enough to be able to steal?"

"Money," Vandaleur said.

"Money for what? Come, my friend, let us exchange confidences. I will tell you why I beg, if you will tell my why you steal. My name is Blenheim."

"My name is . . .Vole."

"I was not begging for sight at St. Paul's, Mr. Vole. I was begging for a number."

"A number?"

"Ah, yes. Numbers rational, numbers irrational. Numbers imaginary. Positive integers. Negative integers. Fractions, positive and negative. Eh? You have never heard of Blenheim's immortal treatise on Twenty Zeros, or The Differences in Absence of Quantity?" Blenheim smiled bitterly. "I am the wizard of the Theory of Numbers, Mr. Vole, and I have exhausted the charm of Number for myself. After fifty years of wizardry, senility approaches and appetite vanishes. I have been praying in St. Paul's for inspiration. Dear God, I prayed, if You exist, send me a Number."

Vandaleur slowly lifted the cardboard portfolio and touched Blenheim's hand with it. "In here," he said, "is a number. A hidden number. A secret number. The number of a crime. Shall we exchange, Mr. Blenheim? Shelter for a number?"

"Neither begging nor stealing, eh?" Blenheim said. "But a bargain. So all life reduces itself to the banal." The sightless eyes again passed over Vandaleur and the android. "Perhaps the Almighty is not God but a merchant. Come home with me."

On the top floor of Blenheim's house we share a room—two beds, two closets, two washstands, one bathroom. Vandaleur bruised my forehead again and sent me out to find work, and while the android worked, I consulted with Blenheim and read him the papers from the portfolio, one by one. All reet! All reet!

Vandaleur told him this much and no more. He was a student, I said, planning a thesis on the murdering android. In these papers which he had collected were the facts that would explain the crimes, of which Blenheim had heard nothing. There must be a correlation, a number, a statistic, something which would account for my derangement, I explained, and Blenheim was piqued by the mystery, the detective story, the human interest of Number.

We examined the papers. As I read them aloud, he listed them and their contents in his blind, meticulous writing. And then I read his notes to him. He listed the papers by type, by type-face, by fact, by fancy, by article, spelling, words, theme, advertising, pictures, subject, politics, prejudices. He analyzed. He studied. He meditated. And we lived together in that top floor, always a little cold, always a little terrified, always a little closer . . . brought together by our fear of us, our hatred between us driven like a wedge into a living tree and splitting the trunk, only to be forever incorporated into the scar tissue. So we grew together; Vandaleur and the android. Be fleet be fleet.

And one afternoon Blenheim called Vandaleur into his study and displayed his notes. "I think I've found it," he said, "but I can't understand it."

Vandaleur's heart leaped.

"Here are the correlations," Blenheim continued. "In fifty papers there are accounts of the criminal android. What is there, outside the depredations, that is also in fifty papers?"

"I don't know, Mr. Blenheim."

"It was a rhetorical question. Here is the answer. The weather."

"What?"

"The weather." Blenheim nodded. "Each crime was committed on a day when the temperature was above ninety degrees Fahrenheit."

"But that's impossible," Vandaleur exclaimed. "It was cold at the university on Lyra Alpha."

"We have no record of any crime committed on Lyra Alpha. There is no paper."

"No. That's right. I—" Vandaleur was confused. Suddenly he exclaimed. "No. You're right. The furnace room. It was hot down there. Hot! Of course. My God, yes! That's the answer. Dallas Brady's electric furnace . . . the rice deltas on Paragon. So jeet your seat. Yes. But why? Why? My God, why?"

I came into the house at that moment and, passing the study, saw Vandaleur and Blenheim. I entered, awaiting commands, my multiple aptitudes devoted to service.

"That's the android, eh?" Blenheim said after a long moment.

"Yes," Vandaleur answered, still confused by the discovery. "And that explains why it refused to attack you that night on the Strand. It wasn't hot enough to break the prime directive. Only in the heat . . . The heat, all reet!" He looked at the android. A lunatic command passed from man to android. I refused. It is forbidden to endanger life. Vandaleur gestured furiously, then seized Blenheim's shoulders and yanked him back out of his desk chair to the floor. Blenheim shouted once. Vandaleur leaped on him like a tiger, pinning him to the floor and sealing his mouth with one hand.

"Find a weapon," I called to the android.

"It is forbidden to endanger life."

"This is a fight for self-preservation. Bring me a weapon!" He held the squirming mathematician with all his weight. I went at once to a cupboard where I knew a revolver was kept. I checked it. It was loaded with five cartridges. I handed it to Vandaleur. I took it, rammed the barrel against Blenheim's head and pulled the trigger. He shuddered once.

We had three hours before the cook returned from her day off. We looted the house. We took Blenheim's money and jewels. We packed a bag with clothes. We took Blenheim's notes, destroyed the newspapers, and we fled, carefully locking the door behind us. In Blenheim's study we left a pile of crumpled papers under a half inch of burning candle. And we soaked the rug around it with kerosene. No, I did all that. The android refused. I am forbidden to endanger life or property.

All reet!

They took the tubes to Leicester Square, changed trains and

rode to the British Museum. There they got off and went to a small Georgian house just off Russell Square. A shingle in the window read: NAN WEBB, PSYCHOMETRIC CONSUL-TANT. Vandaleur had made a note of the address some weeks earlier. They went into the house. The android waited in the foyer with the bag. Vandaleur entered Nan Webb's office.

She was a tall woman with gray shingled hair, very fine English complexion and very bad English legs. Her features were blunt, her expression acute. She nodded to Vandaleur, finished a letter, sealed it and looked up.

"My name," I said, "is Vanderbilt. James Vanderbilt."

"Quite."

"I'm an exchange student at London University."

"Quite."

"I've been researching on the killer android, and I think I've discovered something very interesting. I'd like your advice on it. What is your fee?"

"What is your college at the university?"

"Why?"

"There is a discount for students."

"Merton College."

"That will be two pounds, please."

Vandaleur placed two pounds on the desk and added to the fee Blenheim's notes. "There is a correlation," he said, "between the crimes of the android and the weather. You will note that each crime was committed when the temperature rose above ninety degrees Fahrenheit. Is there a psychometric answer for this?"

Nan Webb nodded, studied the notes for a moment, put down the sheets of paper and said: "Synesthesia, obviously."

"What?"

"Synesthesia," she repeated. "When a sensation, Mr. Van-derbilt, is interpreted immediately in terms of a sensation from a different sense organ than the one stimulated, it is called synesthesia. For example: A sound stimulus gives rise to a simultaneous sensation of definite color. Or color gives rise to a sensation of taste. Or a light stimulus gives rise to a sensation of sound. There can be confusion or short circuiting of any sensation of taste, smell, pain, pressure, temperature and so on. D'you understand?''

''I think so.''

''Your research has probably uncovered the fact that the android most probably reacts to temperature stimulus above the ninety-degree level synesthetically. Most probably there is an endocrine response. Probably a temperature linkage with the android adrenal surrogate. High temperature brings about a response of fear, anger, excitement and violent physical activity . . . all within the province of the adrenal gland.''

''Yes. I see. Then if the android were to be kept in cold climates . . .''

''There would be neither stimulus nor response. There would be no crimes. Quite.''

''I see. What is psychotic projection?''

''How do you mean?''

''Is there any danger of projection with regard to the owner of the android?''

''Very interesting. Projection is a throwing forward. It is the process of throwing out upon another the ideas or impulses that belong to oneself. The paranoid, for example, projects upon others his conflicts and disturbances in order to externalize them. He accuses, directly or by implication, other men of having the very sicknesses with which he is struggling himself.''

''And the danger of projection?''

''It is the danger of the victim's believing what is implied. If you live with a psychotic who projects his sickness upon you, there is a danger of falling into his psychotic pattern and becoming virtually psychotic yourself. As, no doubt, is happening to you, Mr. Vandaleur.''

Vandaleur leaped to his feet.

"You are an ass," Nan Webb went on crisply. She waved the sheets of notes. "This is no exchange student's writing. It's the unique cursive of the famous Blenheim. Every scholar in England knows this blind writing. There is no Merton College at London University. That was a miserable guess. Merton is one of the Oxford Colleges. And you, Mr. Vandaleur, are so obviously infected by association with your deranged android . . . by projection, if you will . . . that I hesitate between calling the Metropolitan Police and the Hospital for the Criminally Insane.''

I took the gun out and shot her.

Reet!

"Antares Two, Alpha Aurigae, Acrux Four, Pollux Nine, Rigel Centaurus," Vandaleur said. "They're all cold. Cold as a witch's kiss. Mean temperatures of forty degrees Fahrenheit. Never get hotter than seventy. We're in business again. Watch that curve.''

The multiple-aptitude android swung the wheel with its accomplished hands. The car took the curve sweetly and sped on through the northern marshes, the reeds stretching for miles, brown and dry, under the cold English sky. The sun was sinking swiftly. Overhead, a lone flight of bustards flapped clumsily eastward. High above the flight, a lone helicopter drifted toward home and warmth.

"No more warmth for us," I said. "No more heat. We're safe when we're cold. We'll hole up in Scotland, make a little money, get across to Norway, build a bankroll and then ship out. We'll settle on Pollux. We're safe. We've licked it. We can live again.''

There was a startling *bleep* from overhead, and then a ragged roar: "ATTENTION JAMES VANDALEUR AND ANDROID. ATTENTION JAMES VANDALEUR AND ANDROID."

Vandaleur started and looked up. The lone helicopter was floating above them. From its belly came amplified commands: "YOU ARE SURROUNDED. THE ROAD IS BLOCKED. YOU ARE TO STOP YOUR CAR AT ONCE AND SUBMIT TO ARREST. STOP AT ONCE!"

I looked at Vandaleur for orders.

"Keep driving," Vandaleur snapped.

The helicopter dropped lower: "ATTENTION ANDROID. YOU ARE IN CONTROL OF THE VEHICLE. YOU ARE TO STOP AT ONCE. THIS IS A STATE DIRECTIVE SUPERSEDING ALL PRIVATE COMMANDS."

The car slowed.

"What the hell are you doing?" I shouted.

"A state directive supercedes all private commands," the android answered. "I must point out to you that—"

"Get the hell away from the wheel," Vandaleur ordered. I clubbed the android, yanked him sideways and squirmed over him to the wheel. The car veered off the road in that moment and went churning through the frozen mud and dry reeds. Vandaleur regained control and continued westward through the marshes toward a parallel highway five miles distant.

"We'll beat their goddamned block," he grunted.

The car pounded and surged. The helicopter dropped even lower. A searchlight blazed from the belly of the plane.

"ATTENTION JAMES VANDALEUR AND ANDROID. SUBMIT TO ARREST. THIS IS A STATE DIRECTIVE SUPERSEDING ALL PRIVATE COMMANDS."

"He can't submit," Vandaleur shouted wildly. "There's no one to submit to. He can't and I won't."

"Christ!" I muttered. "We'll beat them yet. We'll beat the block. We'll beat the heat. We'll—"

"I must point out to you," I said, "that I am required by my prime directive to obey state directives which supersede all private commands. I must submit to arrest."

"Who says it's a state directive?" Vandaleur said. "Them? Up in that plane? They've got to show credentials. They've got to prove it's state authority before you submit. How d'you know they're not crooks trying to trick us?"

Holding the wheel with one arm, he reached into his side pocket to make sure the gun was still in place. The car skidded. The tires squealed on frost and reeds. The wheel was wrenched from his grasp and the car yawed up a small hillock and overturned. The motor roared and the wheels screamed. Vandaleur crawled out and dragged the android with him. For the moment we were outside the cone of light blazing down from the helicopter. We blundered off into the marsh, into the blackness, into concealment... Vandaleur running with a pounding heart, hauling the android along.

The helicopter circled and soared over the wrecked car, searchlight peering, loudspeaker braying. On the highway we had left, lights appeared as the pursuing and blocking parties gathered and followed radio directions from the plane. Vandaleur and the android continued deeper and deeper into the marsh, working their way towards the parallel road and safety. It was night by now. The sky was a black matte. Not a star showed. The temperature was dropping. A southeast night wind knifed us to the bone.

Far behind there was a dull concussion. Vandaleur turned, gasping. The car's fuel had exploded. A geyser of flame shot up like a lurid fountain. It subsided into a low crater of burning reeds. Whipped by the wind, the distant hem of flame fanned up into a wall, ten feet high. The wall began marching down on us, crackling fiercely. Above it, a pall of oily smoke surged forward. Behind it, Vandaleur could make out the figures of men... a mass of beaters searching the marsh.

"Christ!" I cried and searched desperately for safety. He ran, dragging me with him, until their feet crunched through the surface ice of a pool. He trampled the ice furiously, then flung himself down in the numbing water, pulling the android with us.

The wall of flame approached. I could hear the crackle and feel the heat. He could see the searchers clearly. Vandaleur reached into his side pocket for the gun. The pocket was torn. The gun was gone. He groaned and shook with cold and terror. The light from the marsh fire was blinding. Overhead, the helicopter floated helplessly to one side, unable to fly through the smoke and flames and aid the searchers, who were beating far to the right of us.

"They'll miss us," Vandaleur whispered. "Keep quiet. That's an order. They'll miss us. We'll beat them. We'll beat the fire. We'll—"

Three distinct shots sounded less than a hundred feet from the fugitives. *Blam! Blam! Blam!* They came from the last three cartridges in my gun as the marsh fire reached it where it had dropped, and exploded the shells. The searchers turned toward the sound and began working directly toward us. Vandaleur cursed hysterically and tried to submerge even deeper to escape the intolerable heat of the fire. The android began to twitch.

The wall of flame surged up to them. Vandaleur took a deep breath and prepared to submerge until the flame passed over them. The android shuddered and suddenly began to scream.

"All reet! All reet!" it shouted. "Be fleet be fleet!"

"Damn you!" I shouted. I tried to drown the android.

"Damn you!" I cursed. I smashed Vandaleur's face.

The android battered Vandaleur, who fought it off until it burst out of the mud and staggered upright. Before I could return to the attack, the live flames captured it hypnotically. It danced and capered in a lunatic rumba before the wall of fire. Its legs twisted. Its arms waved. The fingers writhed in a private rumba of their own. It shrieked and sang and ran in a crooked waltz before the embrace of the heat, a muddy monster silhouetted against the brilliant sparkling flare.

The searchers shouted. There were shots. The android spun around twice and then continued its horrid dance before the face of the flames. There was a rising gust of wind. The fire swept around the capering figure and enveloped it for a roaring moment. Then the fire swept on, leaving behind it a sobbing mass of synthetic flesh oozing scarlet blood that would never coagulate.

The thermometer would have registered 1200° wondrously Farhenheit.

Vandaleur didn't die. I got away. They missed him while they watched the android caper and die. But I don't know which of us he is these days. Psychotic projection, Wanda warned me. Projection, Nan Webb told him. If you live with a crazy machine long enough, I become crazy too. Reet!

But we know the truth. We know that they were wrong. It was the other way around. It was the man that was corrupting the machine . . . any machine . . . all machines. The new robot and Vandaleur know that because the new robot's started twitching too. Reet!

Here on cold Pollux, the robot is twitching and singing. No heat, but my fingers writhe. No heat, but it's taken the little Talley girl off for a solitary walk. A cheap labor robot. A servo-mechanism . . . all I could afford . . . but it's twitching and humming and walking alone with the child somewhere and I can't find them. Christ! Vandaleur can't find me before it's too late. Cool and discreet, honey, in the dancing frost while the thermometer registers 10° fondly Fahrenheit.

JU